THE GUNSLINGER

Colonel Matt Steadman, cattle-baron of the huge Lazy B ranch, is faced with ruin because of the large-scale rustling operation involving his cattle. The trouble is that the rustlers leave no trace of who they are, nor of their method of moving the cattle. Into this scenario steps the gunfighter called Texas Jake, and immediately things begin to hot up — starting with the mysterious red-headed Judith who is linked with the big Mexican killer Ted Gonzales.

PAT REDFORD

THE GUNSLINGER

Complete and Unabridged

LINFORD
Leicester

First published in Great Britain in 1992 by
Robert Hale Limited
London

First Linford Edition
published 1999
by arrangement with
Robert Hale Limited
London

British Library CIP Data

Redford, Pat
    The gunslinger.—Large print ed.—
    Linford western library
    1. Western stories
    2. Large type books
    I. Title
    823.9′14 [F]

ISBN 0–7089–5554–1

Published by
F. A. Thorpe (Publishing) Ltd.
Anstey, Leicestershire

Set by Words & Graphics Ltd.
Anstey, Leicestershire
Printed and bound in Great Britain by
T. J. International Ltd., Padstow, Cornwall

This book is printed on acid-free paper

1

Above the southern desert of the Arizona territory the pre-dawn sky was pearl-grey; in the air still the last remnants of the night-time cool.

Across the wide, shallow valley, on the far incline, a puff of dust was growing. Texas Jake watched it as it came down the slope. Whoever it was, was on the old coach trail. And coming mighty fast. Too damn fast. No horse could stand that pace, not for long. By the time it reached the incline out of the valley this side, that cowpony would be all but dead on its feet.

Texas Jake looked down at the trail where it topped the rise below him. Would be about there, he reckoned. The horse wouldn't make the rise. Not at that pace. Not a hope o' that!

Suddenly he stiffened. Through the long trail of dust, now hanging thinly in the air over the far incline, another bunch of dust-puffs had made their appearance. Three riders this time, it looked like. And they were gaining on the first, though slowly. They had a long way to catch up.

Once more Jake looked down at the coach-trail topping the rise below him — estimating yet again. Yes, that was the place. It would surely be thereabouts.

In the gully behind him the two horses were grazing. The small seepage-spring was almost dried up, but enough green grass still grew around it. Both animals were already saddled, the pack-animal all loaded up with his bed-roll and supplies.

Jake took another brief look at the dust-clouds. He reckoned he had time — just. Moving down into the gully, he picked up the headstall and clicked his tongue the way the ponies understood. The pack-horse stopped eating, pricked up its ears and waited. Jake felt for its jaw and slipped the bit in. It was a curb-bit, the mildest sort — right for a pack-animal. Then he eased the split-ear headstall on and let the reins hang down. Like that, ground-tied, the horse would stand until the reins were picked up again.

The saddle-horse, watching all this, was less accepting of his bit. It was a spade, a harsh bit, and the horse did not like it — although his rider always worked it with the lightest of touches.

Jake checked the Winchester in its saddle-scabbard, and buckled on another gunbelt. Normally he wore only one, but those dust-clouds looked like trouble. Could be he might just be needing both his single-action Colt .45 Peacemakers this time.

He removed his buckskin gloves and broke open each gun. He spun the cylinder and made sure that the empty safety chamber was now on the last notch; and each hammer had the first full chamber under it. That done, he mounted the saddle-horse and moved over behind a rocky outcrop at the top of the trail.

The riders were much nearer now, already on their way up the slope. Once more Jake stiffened briefly with surprise. Under the first dust-cloud was no rider but a trap, driven by a woman, bare-headed, her long red hair streaming out behind her. There was fear in her face as she belaboured the exhausted horse with her quirt.

The three riders behind were now close to the trap. Intermittently Jake caught a glimpse of one or other of them through the dust-cloud. They had their neckerchiefs pulled up over their mouths and noses, whether in an attempt to hide their identity, or merely because of the dust, Jake had no means of knowing.

The trap-horse was now flagging badly and, more or less at the spot Jake had guessed, the leading rider caught up, leaned over, grabbed the pony's bridle, and brought the trap to a stop.

Fury blazed in the face of the woman. Viciously she swung her quirt. With a quick movement the man took the blow across his shoulders. At the same moment he reached out and tore the quirt from her hand. As he raised it, apparently to bring it down on the woman, Jake moved his horse out from behind the outcrop.

'Keep it just there,' he drawled.

The man, quirt still raised, swung round in the saddle and found himself staring down the barrels of two rock-steady six-guns. For a brief moment he hesitated. Jake moved both guns slightly. The meaning was clear. Slowly the man brought down his quirt arm. He made no other move.

Jake looked at the woman. She was staring at him, still open-mouthed with surprise.

'You're free to go, ma'am,' he said. He let his eyes rest for a moment on the trap-horse. 'But this time you'd better walk that horse o' yours — and slow.'

Still staring at him, she shook her head slowly. All the fight seemed suddenly to have gone out of her.

'No,' she said dully. 'They'll only follow me.'

The hint of a smile touched the Texan's eyes for a brief moment.

'No, ma'am. That they won't. Not unless they aim to walk.'

That seemed to enrage the man with the quirt.

'Horse thief!' he snarled.

He was a big man, a Mexican by the look of him, and he was clearly furiously angry. But he should not have said that. The Texan's eyes hardened and the guns lifted a fraction of an inch.

'No!' shouted the woman, suddenly coming to life. 'No! No! Don't shoot.'

The Texan's voice was soft and cold, and his eyes pure steel.

'No man calls me a horse thief, ma'am — and gets away with it.'

Some of the colour had drained from the face of the Mexican.

'He didn't mean it!' insisted the woman. 'Ted, tell him you didn't mean it!'

She was pleading the man's case — vehemently, desperate. What the hell was going on?

'Look,' she said, urgent, desperate, 'it's my fault. It's all my fault. I shouldn't have done it. These men know I shouldn't have done it. They came to help me, to take me back.'

She swung round suddenly to the Mexican.

'Ted, turn the horse for me. I want to go back.'

Her voice was now imperious, demanding.

Slowly the Mexican turned his horse and faced Jake. Very gently, with finger and thumb only, he pulled the gun from the holster on his hip and let it fall to the ground. Then he leaned forward and spoke softly.

'You shoot,' he said. 'You shoot. You kill unarmed man. For that, out here, *hombre*, you hang.'

He had evaded the threat to his life — evaded it in a most cowardly, but a most effective way.

The Texan's fury turned to cold contempt.

'Get moving!' was all he said — with a snap.

Swiftly the Mexican turned his horse, reached down for the bridle, and pulled the trap-pony round to face back the way it had come.

As they moved off at a walk, not one of them — not the woman or any of the three men — made the slightest attempt to look back.

Texas Jake holstered his six-guns and looked down frowning at the Mexican's gun lying there, where it had fallen, in the dust of the coach-trail.

There was something wrong in that outfit — something mighty wrong!

★ ★ ★

It was getting on for midday when Texas Jake, walking his horses through

8

the shimmering heat, reached the little town of El Pueblo. The whittlers and the tobacco-chewers on the boardwalk outside the saloon watched his progress down the street to Dave's Rooming House, watched him dismount, loop the reins over the hitching rail and go into the low adobe building.

At that point Pigtoed Pete expelled a long reflective squirt of juice into the road, levered himself up off the boardwalk, hitched his belt, squinted up at the sun, pushed his hat forward over his eyes, and ambled off to the marshal's office up the road.

Marshal Birch was a small man with a big moustache. He had his feet up on the desk and his hands behind his head as he leaned back in his chair. He opened one eye and squinted at Pigtoed Pete.

'What's news, Pete?'

Pete sat himself down across the desk from the marshal.

'Don't rightly know, marshal, if it's news. Or if it ain't.'

The marshal opened the other eye and waited.

'Stranger in town,' said Pete.

The marshal closed his eyes again.

'Well?' he said.

'Tall feller,' said Pete. 'Two horses.'

'Range hand?'

Pete shook his head.

'Don't look that way.'

The marshal opened his eyes again.

'Ain't wearing chaps,' said Pete, scratching his ear. 'Wears two guns.'

The marshal took his feet off the desk and sat up.

'So?'

'Two guns,' said Pete, scratching his chin this time. 'Low down, tied.'

He looked at the marshal, who was frowning now.

'Sloping,' said Pete.

He made a motion with his two hands of a pair of six-guns, butts facing back, but muzzles also inclined slightly backward — for a quick draw.

'Gunslinger,' said the marshal with a heavy sigh.

Pete gave another scratch to his chin.

'Looks that way,' he said.

He thought a while.

'Yeah,' he said eventually. 'Sure looks that way. I'll wager them guns is on hair-triggers — and their sights is all filed down.'

The marshal was looking worried.

'What's he after, Pete? Any ideas?'

Pete gave a wolfish grin, showing his remaining teeth, brown-stained by tobacco.

'Right now I reckon he's after a bath at Dave's — and a bed for tonight.'

'Mebbe,' said the marshal hopefully, 'he's just passing through.'

Pete's grin widened.

'Mebbe,' he said.

But there was no conviction in the word.

★ ★ ★

The crudely written board said merely 'Pablo's'. Texas Jake, the trail-dust all washed off him, and comfortable in the clean new shirt from the general store alongside Dave's Rooming House, looked at the sign, pushed open the door, and walked in.

The place was empty, except for the flies, but filled with the sharp delicious smell of Mexican cooking. Jake sat himself down at a small table and waited. Presently the bead curtain over the inner doorway parted and a short fat man emerged, wiping his lips.

'You will eat, *señor*?'

Jake nodded.

'What you got? Tamales?'

'Si, si. Tamales, tortillas, carne con chili, anything.'

'Tamales will do.'

That must have been what the man was eating, because in a couple of minutes he was back with the food. Jake tried it.

'Good,' he said.

'You know Mexican food, *señor*?'

Jake nodded.

'Most Americanos don't like.'

He had nearly said 'gringos', but had stopped himself in time.

Jake said, 'You Pablo?'

The man nodded.

'Been long here — in this town?'

'Long, yes. Long time. Three, four years.'

'Know all the Mexicans round here?'

A suspicious look came over the man's face.

'Know some, mebbe,' he said cautiously.

'Big fellow,' said Jake. 'Heavy moustache. Works on a ranch somewhere here.'

The eating-house proprietor shrugged.

'Could be anybody,' he said, relieved. 'Ten, twenty men — anybody.'

'Broken tooth,' said Jake, pointing to his own tooth.

Again the fat man shrugged, but his eyes were uncomfortable.

'Name of Ted,' said Jake.

The man pulled a rag from his pocket and suddenly found something to rub on the edge of the table. He began to shake his head.

'So you do know him,' said Jake.

The proprietor looked unhappy.

'Bad man,' he muttered, before he could stop himself. 'Dangerous. Very dangerous. Bad man to fight. Always wins — *por fin*, in the end.'

'He didn't win today.'

The little fat man shrugged.

'There is tomorrow. And next day.'

'Ted who?'

'Gonzales. Ted Gonzales. Works for Colonel Steadman. Foreman. Big ranch, way out.'

Suddenly he leaned forward and, glancing round to make sure there was nobody to overhear him, spoke quickly and softly to Jake.

'You no tell,' he said urgently. 'You no tell Pablo tell you. Ted Gonzales, he fighter. He kill men — many men.'

'How?' said Jake contemptuously. 'By dropping his gun in the dirt?'

To Jake's surprise the Mexican nodded vigorously.

'Si, si! That way. Drops gun. Other

man put away gun. Ted kill him. With knife. Always with knife.'

'Thrown?'

'Si, si! Throw knife. Never miss.'

Texas Jake smiled slightly.

'I sure will have to remember that,' he said softly.

★ ★ ★

Marshal Birch was not a happy man. He was a man of peace, and he wore his marshal's badge with reluctance. He liked to think of the six-gun at his hip more as a symbol than a weapon, although when it came to the crunch he could use the iron with tolerable competence. But it was his skill in settling squabbles amicably that had originally caused the few remaining citizens of El Pueblo to press him into service as their marshal.

For El Pueblo had little need of a gun-toting fast-drawing lawman. About the only shooting that ever happened there was when a couple of Colonel

15

Steadman's hands, high on tequila, raced down the main (and only) street, shooting at the sky. And even that large target they were likely to miss — and damage themselves instead.

But now suddenly there was a professional gunslinger in town — a hired killer, by the look of him. The marshal frowned, sighed, took his feet off the desk, settled his hat more firmly on his head, buckled on his gunbelt, and set off for the saloon.

There, as he had expected, he found Happy Harry playing poker with a couple of other hands from the Steadman outfit. Marshal Birch found a chair, reversed it, leaned his forearms on the chair-back, and watched the play.

The players nodded at him briefly, or said howdee, while they concentrated on their game. But Harry was curious. The marshal never played cards. He had something on his mind. So, when the game was finished, Happy Harry threw in his hand and looked across.

'Beer, marshal?'

The marshal nodded and got up, and the two men ambled over to the bar. Even then it was a while before Marshal Birch had anything to say. Then he turned his beer round thoughtfully and looked at it.

'Colonel expecting visitors?'

'Nope.'

The marshal turned his beer round some more.

'Looks he's got one.'

Harry nodded. He knew about the stranger in town. Everybody knew by now.

'Could be, at that.'

He looked at the marshal.

'You aim to raise a posse?'

The marshal shook his head.

'No proof,' he said. 'Yet.'

Harry nodded. That was the marshal's way. Wait till you know — for sure. No lynching the wrong man. He would let the man ride out to the Colonel's outfit, let him make his play, even. And then . . .

17

'We hanged the last one,' said Harry, ruminatively.

The marshal nodded.

'You boys leaving in the morning?'

'Yep.'

The marshal looked thoughtfully at Harry.

'Keep it out of town,' he said.

'We always do,' said Happy Harry.

There was steel in his voice.

The marshal drank down the rest of his beer, nodded to Happy Harry, and walked out of the saloon. Out in the sunshine on the boardwalk he hesitated a moment, then drifted casually down the road.

At the livery-barn the dayman was idly busy with small chores. He greeted the marshal with curiosity. The marshal's horse, after all, was stabled behind his own house. The marshal ignored the dayman's curiosity and drifted into the barn.

That day the livery-barn had few customers, and the stranger's saddles were immediately noticeable on their saddle-poles. Marshal Birch examined them with interest, starting with the older Texas saddle, almost bare of leather, but double-cinched. This would be the one for the pony acting as pack-horse, he reckoned. The other saddle was the newfangled Denver version, also double-cinched, but all leather, with a good horn and a long skirt. A strong roping saddle that one, one coming to be much favoured by Texans, but heavy — a good forty pounds. Neither saddle had thorn-protective tapaderos on the strong, steambent wooden stirrups.

The marshal wandered out to the corral, where the horses were switching their tails against the flies. He leaned on the rail and watched the little pack-horse pretending to be unaware of his presence. The dayman joined him at the railings and, noticing his interest in the small horse, delivered himself of the opinion he had formed while handling the horse.

'That there's a cuttin'-horse if ever

I saw one. Smart little twister.'

A cutting-horse, a good one, could cut a Texas Longhorn out of the herd almost by himself. His rider had merely to point him at the right animal.

'Quarter-horse?' asked the marshal, with curiosity.

A quarter-horse was quick, but only in short bursts.

'Nah,' said the dayman with disgust. 'Quarter-horse ain't got no stamina. Reckon this one's got plenty.'

The marshal turned his gaze on the stranger's riding-horse. A bigger horse this, strong, a stayer.

'What's he wearing?' asked the marshal, suddenly thoughtful.

'The stranger?' The dayman shrugged. 'The usual — more or less.'

'How much more — and how much less?'

'Wal, lessee,' the dayman brooded. 'I reckon he's Texan, but he don't wear no ten-gallon job.'

'What, then?'

'Flat-top.'

He meant the wide-brimmed low-crown plainsman's hat. The low crown made it easier to keep it on in the constant plains wind.

'Spurs?'

'Ah! Fancy, them. Real fancy. Silver. Heel-chain, jingle-bobs — all fancy. Like a whole musical band walkin' along.'

'Rowels? Spiked?'

'Nah. No spikes. Filed down. Wouldn't even prick a horse. Nah, all show.'

The marshal turned away. Strange. A man who dressed like a cowhand, but clearly wasn't one. He swung round on the dayman.

'What's his rope?'

'Sixty-foot rawhide lariat, horn honda. But there's a grass rope, too. On the other saddle. Short. Thirty, forty foot.'

The marshal frowned.

'He wear gloves?'

'Sure. Real fancy ones. Soft buckskin. Must have cost him. But he needs them gloves. Needs 'em real bad.'

The marshal raised his eyebrows.

'Soft hands?'

'Soft as a baby's.'

The marshal sighed gloomily. In that world only two types of men had soft hands. One lot were gamblers and card-sharps. The other lot were gunmen — professional killers.

There was no doubt to which lot this stranger belonged.

★ ★ ★

Coming into the saloon out of the heat and the bright sunlight, Texas Jake paused a moment to allow his eyes to get used to the gloom. Then he moved over to the bar and ordered a beer. The saloon was almost empty, but at the far end four men were playing cards. With his habitual caution, Jake took note of them without seeming to do so, and took care to stand at the bar so that they were still within the edge of his field of vision. They appeared to be ordinary cowhands, and the guns they

22

carried were belted on with the usual rangehand's casual carelessness. They were a little drunk already, probably on the beer they were drinking, but none of them seemed particularly rowdy. Jake realized that they were very much aware of his entry, though they gave no sign.

The saloon-keeper was curious about Jake. That was clear. He was also well aware of the western code — no questions. Jake decided to make his play. He raised his voice slightly, so that the card-players could hear.

'Colonel Steadman,' said Jake to the saloon-keeper.

Jake was immediately aware of an instant silence among the players, and four heads turning in his direction. The saloon-keeper was waiting for the rest of the question. His look was guarded.

'He live around here?'

Jake's voice was casual, curious.

'Sure,' said the saloon-keeper, making sure that the card-players could hear.

'Got a ranch. About ten miles out. Lazy B. Biggest outfit in these parts.'

The card-players had risen by now and drifted over to the bar. It was Happy Harry who spoke next.

'Got business with Colonel Steadman?'

The words were casual enough, but the expressions on the four faces in the semicircle around Jake were tight and grim.

'Yep,' said Jake casually. 'Got a letter for him.'

They watched him in silence: tense, disbelieving. With two fingers extended, Jake slowly moved his hand up to the pocket in his vest. Inserting the two fingers, he came up with a sealed letter, which he held up for them all to see. 'To Colonel Steadman,' the outer covering read. 'To be delivered by the hand of Texas Jake. Personal and private'.

Happy Harry, his face still grim and taut, extended his hand.

'I'll take that to the colonel,' he said.

It was a direct challenge. Immediately there was heightened tension among the four. But Jake remained casual. Still with only two fingers, he pushed the letter back into his vest-pocket.

'It says on the letter,' he drawled, ' 'to be delivered by the hand of Texas Jake'. That's me. But I'll tell you what. I'll be right glad of the company of you and the boys on my ride out to the Lazy B in the morning.'

It was a conciliatory offer, one that allowed Happy Harry to withdraw without loss of face. He nodded curtly.

'Four o'clock, then,' he said tersely. 'Outside the livery-barn.'

With that, he and the others turned abruptly and made their way back to the card-table. Texas Jake finished his beer, nodded to the saloon-keeper, and drifted back out into the sunshine and the heat.

He had taken the first step. Tomorrow he would take the next one.

2

They set off in the first post-dawn flush of light, with the sun, huge and red, creeping slowly up out of the eastern desert — that most peaceful time of the day, when the world seemed to hold its breath in a momentary hiatus.

There were only four of them, Jake included. The other, Jake surmised, had ridden ahead to warn the colonel of his coming.

About fifteen miles or so in the distance the perpendicular walls of the Gran Mesa reared up out of the flat horizon. Somewhere in that great arid wall, around the side away from them, was the narrow cleft that gave access to the canyon of the Palo Verde creek.

This wondrous, life-giving stream came out of the rock in a spring at one end of the valley and meandered down between banks of rich grass and clumps of trees to the wide shallow lake at the other end, before it dipped down underground again and disappeared into the bowels of the earth beneath the mesa.

Some four or five years ago Matt Steadman had found this place. Before then it had been wild — a site used only by the Mexican comancheros, and the Indians with whom they traded in stolen cattle.

Matt had been ranching and doing well in Texas before the crash of '73 had brought him and so many others down. With everything lost — except for 500 cattle he was able to rescue from the catastrophe — he had looked around for a new place in a new part of the country, from which to start up again — and had found the Palo Verde.

Half the canyons in the south west were Palo this or Palo that, and not a few were green enough to merit the name Palo Verde — the Green Wood.

But this particular canyon was something special. You could have put a whole town in it — even two towns! It had water, sweet water, and grass enough for thousands of beeves. Above all, it was a natural huge corral, with only one entrance, through a narrow defile, and with a sheer rock-face all the way round.

No need to ride line here! No need at round-up time to have to sort out other men's mavericks! No need even for the new fangled barbed-wire fencing that Matt had heard so many rumours of! It had all been taken care of by mother nature!

There was another great advantage in having such a natural closed-off range.

Now, Matt realized, he could bring in imported bulls from England and Scotland to improve the tough, stringy meat of the Texas Longhorns — bulls that could not simply wander off and impregnate other men's cows!

He could try Aberdeen Angus, or Durham Shorthorns, or Herefords. Yes, above all, Herefords — those 'White Faces' that cowmen were finding settled in so well and made such a difference to the slaughter-stock.

There was only one thing that he still needed in order to make all this come true — money!

Fortunately, it was a time when rich men in the east — and even as far afield as England and Scotland and Ireland — were looking around for new fields of investment.

Not a few had been attracted by the romantic tales that they had been fed about cattle-ranching on the frontiers of the Wild West, and not a few had taken a long hard look beneath the romance and found the facts promising.

English, Scots and Irish money — and money from the United States east coast — suddenly began to flood into the cattle-ranching business. Matt pulled his hat down firmly on his head and set off for the east coast — to find a backer.

He found one, and quicker than

he had expected.

James Longlater was a wealthy New Englander, related to some of the leading families on the east coast. The idea of being part-owner of a cattle ranch in the Arizona Territory appealed to the romantic in him. He came out, looked over the Palo Verde, immediately recognized its advantages, and a deal was quickly struck.

For three years Matt would receive a salary as manager, and James Longlater would provide the considerable sums necessary for the purchase of stock and the improvement of the herd. After that, Matt was to pay back a proportion of the investment out of profits, and was himself to take a part share in the business. It all seemed too good to be true!

For the first two or three years things had gone well. Matt had purchased more and more stock, and brought in Hereford bulls to improve the herd. The enterprise was on the verge of beginning to show a profit, and the future looked more than rosy.

Then suddenly, somehow, for no reason, everything had started to go wrong. It had begun with a quarrel that blew up with another cattle baron some fifty miles from Palo Verde. The man's name was Lew Gardiner, and it was a dispute over nothing — some steers shipped from a railhead — a trivial matter of not the slightest importance.

But from then on nothing seemed to go right at Palo Verde. Some of the cattle developed Texas fever, and an inordinate amount of screw-worm began to plague the herd. A prize Hereford bull, bought at great expense, managed to get himself bogged down at the edge of the lake and drowned, and one of the range riders was careless enough to be gored by an irate Longhorn steer.

Most ominous of all, Matt Steadman became convinced that somebody was out to get him.

The first indication of that had been a rifle bullet which narrowly missed him one evening on the way back to Palo Verde from El Pueblo. He had been unable to identify the source of the shot, and the sudden coming of nightfall had precluded any attempt at a search.

The next occasion had been when a stranger was found skulking in the canyon itself, laid-up all ready to dry-gulch him as he came past.

They had wasted no time with that one! The boys had strung him up at once — even before Marshal Birch and his posse could get there.

So Matt was wary, suspicious of all strangers, cautious even in his own canyon.

It was a wariness and caution — mixed now with rage — that grew even greater when he realized that he was being robbed. His cattle were being rustled — and not merely in ones and twos, but literally in droves — to such an extent that it would not be much longer before the entire valley was cleaned out!

The trouble was that — unbelievably — he could not figure out how it was being done — *how* the cattle were being got out of the valley.

He and his men had watched and searched — and searched and watched. But they had come up with absolutely nothing, not even the faintest hint of an explanation.

It was utterly baffling. Matt Steadman was at his wits' end.

Or so the story went, at least — as Texas Jake had been told it.

★ ★ ★

The defile giving access to the Palo Verde canyon was so narrow that they had to ride in single file between the towering rocky walls — Happy Harry in the lead, then Jake, then the two others.

Texas Jake was aware now of a new alertness in his companions, an extra tautness, a tension of nerves — and a renewed hard grimness of countenance.

33

Things, he realized, were about to come to a head.

Suddenly the narrow darkness of the defile gave way to the open sunlight of the valley. Here, with the towering rock-ramparts running down the sides of the enclosure and widening out as they went, there were trees on the slopes, and greensward, and the musical gurgle of the spring coming from the mountainside — a bubbling of clear, sweet water, cleaned by its journey along the subterranean strata under the Mesa, its purity protected here at its source from contamination by cattle, with a stoutly built log fence.

Texas Jake took in the scene with a couple of swift glances, but his main attention was on the buildings ahead — the small ranch house, surrounded by the usual cookhouse, bunk house, barns and corral for the horses.

On the porch of the ranch house the large figure of a man awaited Jake — feet apart, jaw thrust forward, a shotgun in his hands. Before him, in front of the porch, lounged a couple of cowhands, their relaxed pose contradicted by the grim tension in their faces. Jake recognized one of them as the third of Happy Harry's companions of the night before.

The four horses slowed to a walk, and spread out, leaving Jake centre-stage facing the colonel.

'That's far enough!' barked Matt Steadman. 'Hold it right there!'

And the barrels of the shotgun came up threateningly.

Jake brought his horses to a stop and folded his hands over the saddle-horn.

'You Colonel Steadman?'

He made the question a relaxed, casual drawl.

'I am,' snapped the colonel. 'And what of it?'

'Got a letter for you,' said Jake, keeping his hands on the saddle-horn.

'Letter be damned. Any fool can think up a letter. What's your purpose coming here?'

His voice was harsh and suspicious. But Jake seemed in no hurry to answer. The shotgun barrels moved up another inch.

'My purpose coming here?' Again it was a casual drawl. 'Why, I reckon that's all most likely taken care of in the letter.'

'Damn your letter!' snarled Matt Steadman. '*You* tell me!'

Slowly Jake shook his head.

'You'd better read the letter,' he said.

For a brief moment he wondered if he had chanced things too far. The barrels of the shotgun moved up slightly. This was the moment his life hung by a hair — and the moment seemed to last for ever. All he could do was to maintain his pose of relaxed casualness and, above all, keep his hands, still gloved, casually folded on his saddle-horn. The slightest tensing up on his part, he felt sure, could quite easily result in the paranoia of the big man before him taking over and blasting him out of the saddle.

The seconds ticked by. The colonel was clearly in two minds. Then the shotgun barrels came down slightly.

'Where's the letter?'

Inwardly Jake breathed a sigh of relief. Outwardly he did not move a muscle.

'In my vest-pocket,' he said, careful still not to move his hands.

'Take it out,' snapped the colonel. 'But you had better do it slow — damned slow!'

The muzzles of the shotgun came up again. Slowly, very slowly, Jake raised both hands above the level of his forehead. Slowly, very slowly, his left hand began to ease the glove off the right hand. When that was done he closed the now naked right hand, leaving only forefinger and middle finger extended. These, still extended, he inverted and moved slowly down towards his breast pocket, reaching into it with the two fingers, and coming up with the letter between them. Still holding the letter like that, he turned it face-on to the colonel and waited.

'Hand it to Harry,' said Matt Steadman.

Jake remained motionless. Happy Harry sidled his horse over, reached across, took the letter, and walked his horse round in a half circle, out of the line of fire, to hand the letter up to the man on the porch.

Jake slowly put his hands back on the saddle-horn and waited. Still watching Jake, and still succeeding in keeping the shotgun pointed, the colonel managed clumsily, with one hand and the aid of his teeth, to open the sealed piece of paper.

Holding it up to one side before his face, so that Jake was not out of his line of vision, he flicked his eyes over the note. Then he read it again, slowly this time.

As the colonel read the letter for the third time, with concentration now, the barrels of the shotgun began to come down — right down. He cradled the shotgun under his arm, barrels pointing down to the ground, folded the letter carefully, and put it in his pocket. Only then did he look up at Jake.

'You Texas Jake?'

His voice was now quiet, deliberate, thoughtful — quite different from the snarling, edgy suspicion of only a few moments ago.

'Sure am,' said Jake.

All the time that the dramatic change had come over the colonel, Jake had continued in his pose of casual relaxation, carefully remaining unmoving in his saddle, and careful that his hands — the one gloved, and the other still ungloved — stayed absolutely still on his saddle-horn.

The colonel nodded.

'Get yourself a place in the bunk house,' he said curtly, 'and settle in. Harry'll show you where.'

With that he turned on his heel and strode back inside the ranch house.

Suddenly all the tension had gone out of the scene. The two cowboys in front of the porch sloped off back to their chores. Happy Harry and his two companions began to move their horses over to the corral, and Texas Jake moved his mounts to follow. Inwardly, despite his narrow scrape, he was smiling. He had taken the second step. But from now on it was going to get a lot harder.

★ ★ ★

Jake was busy slopping water from the tub over his face and neck to get rid of some of the dust from his morning ride, when Happy Harry came up. The two horses had been off-saddled and were in the corral, and Jake's bed-roll, with the saddles, was on the sward outside the bunk house. With the weather dry and fine the way it was, there was no sense in picking up the bugs and lice so usual in ranch bunk houses. Like the other hands, he would sleep out under the stars.

Happy Harry no longer had the taut

grim expression with which he had faced Jake in the bar in El Pueblo the previous day. Now, instead, his eyes had the ghost of a twinkle, and his mouth the only half-hidden hint of a smile. It was easy to see where he had got his nickname from. He seemed to be one of those naturally cheerful people always prepared to look on the bright side of events. And yet, with all that, his eyes still had a wary look to them — and a look of downright curiosity.

'Boss-man's hollering for you,' he said, watching Jake drying off some of the water from his hair. 'That letter o' your'n sure made him turn turtle.'

It was as far as convention permitted him to go in trying to satisfy his curiosity. He knew better than to ask outright what was going on. But Jake was not in the game of satisfying idle curiosity — Happy Harry's or anyone else's.

'Sure did,' he agreed, without amplification.

'Never seen him change mood that fast. Never.'

But Jake was not to be drawn.

'Where is he?' he asked. 'Ranch house?'

'Sure thing. Up the steps to the porch, in the door, then first right. You'll likely find him there, at his desk.'

Jake nodded his thanks, finished drying his hair, put a comb through it before he put his hat back on, shook out his shirt and got into it. Then he stepped out for the ranch house, feeling absurdly light without the weight of his six-guns and shell-belt. They were all safely wrapped up in his bed-roll.

Harry had been right. Matt Steadman was at his desk. He looked up as Jake knocked briefly and walked in.

'Sit down,' he said. 'Be with you in a minute.'

While the colonel finished the letter he was writing, Jake made himself comfortable in an armchair and looked round the room.

Some care had been taken in the furnishing, he noticed. The room was not the normal cattleman's office-cum-sitting-room. There were no spittoons, and no clutter. Furthermore the room was clean as well as tidy, the wood polished to a shine; pictures on the walls; vases, figurines and other ornaments. It may have been the office of a cattleman, but it was also a parlour — managed by the hand of a woman.

After a minute or so, the colonel sealed his letter and came over to Jake. There was no welcome in his face, and his eyes were hard and sharp, but his apology was handsome enough.

'I owe you an explanation,' he said curtly, sitting down in the chair opposite Jake. 'If you had sent word who the letter was from, you would have had a more civil reception.'

'Thought you'd better read that for yourself,' said Jake laconically.

The hard, sharp gaze did not change, though the colonel's words were simple enough, if a little stark.

'That could have cost you your life,' he said. He hesitated. 'There's somebody,' he said eventually, speaking slowly and deliberately, 'who's out to get me — and has almost succeeded, several times. It has been pure chance, luck, that I have escaped up till now. That is why I am more than a little suspicious of all visitors I do not know. The last attempt was by a stranger posing as a visitor.'

A grim smile broke momentarily through the harshness of his countenance.

'He, too, was carrying a letter. I was almost taken in. If he had been a better shot . . . '

He left it there, and Jake wondered what had happened to the man. Shot or hanged, he guessed. But he did not ask. He began to realize how narrow his own escape had been.

Having got all that off his chest, Matt Steadman was almost half way to cheering up.

'Well,' he said, with a finality which

seemed to say that the previous subject was now disposed of, 'what say we have some coffee before we get down to business?'

'That,' said Jake, just beginning to realize that coffee would be exactly what he wanted at the moment, 'would suit me fine.'

'And it won't be Arbuckle's,' said the colonel with a grim smile, referring to the brand most popular with range riders. 'Something better. Much better.'

He got up and left the room. When he returned some minutes later he was followed by a woman carrying a tray of coffee. Suddenly the aroma of the beverage filled the room deliciously, and Jake was immediately aware that indeed it was not Arbuckle's, but something rather more exotic.

However, all this he noticed by the way, in passing. His attention was riveted on the young woman carrying the tray — on her hauteur, and the elegance of her clothing, but above all on the beautiful cascade of her long red hair falling over her shoulders and down her back. It was the young woman in the trap the previous morning — the woman who had been fleeing in fear from Ted Gonzales and his two range hands.

'This,' said Matt Steadman curtly, 'is my daughter Judith. Texas Jake.'

Jake stood up.

'Pleased to make your acquaintance, ma'am,' he said.

Her bold eyes turned on him, as to a complete stranger. She inclined her head in acknowledgement of his greeting.

'Mr Jake,' she said formally.

'Jake, ma'am. Just Jake. Texas Jake.'

She smiled slightly.

'You are really from Texas?'

'Sure am, ma'am. San Anton'.'

Not a hint that she had ever seen him before anywhere. He watched her as she went about serving the coffee, but she did not glance in his direction again, and when she had finished what she was doing she went out of the room and left the two men to the business they had to discuss.

'This letter you brought,' said Matt at last, thoughtfully, 'is from my partner, James Longlater. But then I don't have to tell you that.'

Texas Jake nodded. Matt looked hard at him.

'He tells me that he has hired you.'

Again Jake nodded. 'He says you are losing cattle,' he said. 'That's my job — finding out why people lose cattle, and who is taking them. That's what he hired me for.'

Matt Steadman gave Jake another long, hard look.

'When do you start?' he said at last.

Jake took the last couple of mouthfuls of his coffee. Then he stood up.

'Now,' he said. 'Right away.'

★ ★ ★

Standing at the window, Matt Steadman watched Jake as he strode towards the bunk house, and his bed-roll on the greensward before it.

No range hand's bandy-legged waddle that, reflected Matt. It was the walk of an active, athletic man. He frowned.

Behind him there was the slight creak of a floorboard. Matt's frown deepened.

'You can come out from behind that door,' he said tersely, without turning round.

For a moment there was a pause. Then Judith appeared round the door and walked into the room. Her chin was up, and there was nothing apologetic about her mien.

'I've told you before,' growled Matt, turning round to scowl at her, 'to keep yourself out of my business.'

'I'm not interfering in your business,' she replied curtly.

'You were listening — behind that door,' snapped her father angrily.

'So?'

'I've told you,' he said deliberately, 'I don't want you involved in any way.'

'Involved?' she snapped angrily. 'With what?'

But Matt just shook his head.

'Something you're ashamed of? Something dishonest even — perhaps?'

Again Matt shook his head.

'Dangerous,' he said. 'Just dangerous. That's why I want you to keep out of it.'

She looked at him grimly.

'Someone is trying to kill you. The same persons — or others — are rustling your cattle. If things go on like this for very much longer you will be either ruined — or dead. How the hell do you expect me to keep out of all that?'

Gloomily Matt looked at her.

'You can't help,' he said.

'Then who can?' snapped Judith angrily. 'This man Texas Jake? Do you expect *him* to solve things for you — on his *own*?'

The colonel looked up at his daughter.

'No,' he said slowly. 'No, I don't expect him to solve anything for me.'

He paused and looked down.

'I don't,' he said quietly, 'expect him to live long enough for that.'

3

The trees were small and wide-spaced, allowing the hot sunlight through in patches to dapple the shade. Jake walked his horses along the narrow game trail towards a little clearing where the grass was green and a minute spring trickled its water reluctantly from the rock face of the canyon wall into a shallow, gravelly pool.

He was riding the smaller of his two horses for a change. Just before he reached the clearing, the horse shied suddenly and began to back nervously away. Jake had no need to ask the reason for this. The soft whirring sound of the rattle-snake had struck his ear simultaneously with the first movement of the horse.

Carefully he backed the horses away. They were nervous — nostrils twitching and ears erect — so he made their reins fast to a small tree and went in search of the snake. Rattlers, Jake knew, like all adders, were only dangerous because they were so slow-moving that they had little time to escape before being trodden on — or being rolled on by a sleeper when they had slid into his bed-roll for warmth.

He found the snake, a large one, coiled up, its head pulled back to lie in the centre of the coil, ready to strike, its rattle whirring away. Pinning the reptile's neck down with a forked stick, Jake sliced off the head with one stroke of his heavy hunting-knife.

For a while the headless body jerked and twisted while the rattle still whirred away. Then the movement subsided and Jake picked up the body by the tail. It was heavy enough for more than a few meals. Rattler steaks made good eating. He had learned that in his hunting days.

Untying the horses, Jake hobbled them and removed their headstalls, leaving them free to graze. Then he began to prepare his meal, his stomach reminding him suddenly that he had not eaten since the previous evening.

The snake he skinned expertly, cutting off the tail and pulling the skin off like a sleeve — the way he had been taught by Old Piute, the Indian, in those long-ago hunting days. He then sliced up the meat, impaled it on pointed sticks, and set the lot to grill over a small fire.

He was a mile or two from the ranch house, and out of its sight, and anyway there was no particular reason to conceal his presence. Nevertheless, with his habitual caution, Jake chose dry twigs, to give a smokeless fire, and kept his ears alert for unusual sounds, pausing every now and then to listen with concentration — almost as if he were expecting someone.

The first sound, when it came, was so faint he almost missed it. It was the faraway clink of horseshoe on stone.

Jake untied the safety strap that held his Colt in its holster, made sure that the gun could move in and out of the leather without hindrance, spun the chamber to leave the empty space at the end, and moved quickly among the trees bordering the game trail, back along the way he had come.

After a short distance Jake selected a suitable spot alongside the trail, concealed himself behind a rocky outcrop, and waited.

The rider was nearer now, the sound of stones being kicked up by the horse more frequent. Jake drew out his Colt. At the same moment the rider came into full view. It was Judith.

Still Jake made no move, concentrating instead on the trail behind her. Only when he was sure, after some time, that nobody was following her, did he holster his gun and make his way back to the camp fire.

There Judith was already trying one of the adder steaks. Looking up, she gestured at the meat.

'Nice.'

Jake nodded.

'What is it? Rabbit?'

Jake pointed at the snake skin, now inside out, salted, and held taut by two U-shaped green twigs, one at either end.

Judith pulled a face.

'Rattler?'

'Sure.'

'Ugh!'

She examined the meat.

'Tastes a bit like chicken.'

She took another bite of meat and looked at Jake.

'Back at the ranch house I thought for a moment that you were going to give me away.'

There was open curiosity in her gaze.

'Why didn't you? I mean, what held you back?'

Jake shrugged.

'It was none of my business.'

She inclined her head.

'Nevertheless . . . ' She hesitated, reluctant it seemed to complete the sentence. 'I was running away,' she added simply.

'From your father?'

She shook her head.

'From everything.'

Jake looked at her thoughtfully.

'Ted Gonzales . . . '

Immediately she made her face expressionless. It was a conscious, deliberate effort.

'What about him?'

Her voice was carefully casual.

'He was not there, at the ranch house.'

She shook her head.

'He's around.'

Suddenly she stood up and faced him fully, the words pouring out of her, full of suppressed fierce urgency.

'Go! Go back! Now! While you still have a chance!'

Jake lifted an ironic eyebrow.

'And the missing cattle?'

Her impatience was fierce.

'To hell with them!'

She shook her head in angry frustration.

'You won't find them! Or who's

doing it, or how! You won't find out because they won't let you!'

'They? Ted Gonzales perhaps?'

Impatiently, fiercely, she shook her head.

'Does it matter? Ted or anyone else. What's the difference?'

She looked at him grimly.

'They killed the last one James sent.'

There was distress in her face.

Jake nodded grimly.

'I know.'

'And they're going to kill you!'

'They can try.'

He was smiling as he said that. But it was a smile that stayed only on his lips. It never reached his eyes.

★ ★ ★

The canyon wall was high — and solid all the way along that side of the valley. Well, almost solid. There were gulches, coulees, washes, draws — some going deep into the mesa, some only shallow, but all of them, deep or shallow, ending

57

up in a blank wall.

That Jake knew already — because he had been told so. There was no way out of this valley, this side or the other, or at the lake end — absolutely no way out at all. Only at the narrow, the ranch house end, was there a way in and out of the canyon — the defile by which they had entered that morning.

And yet cattle were still being rustled — steadily, continuously, and by the hundred!

There were only two possibilities. One was that the beasts were being taken out past the ranch house, in full view, day or night, of everybody in the ranch house, including Matt Steadman and Judith, the cook, and whatever ranch hands were around at the time.

That option Jake ruled out immediately. There would have to be far too many people in the know — let alone the assumption of Matt Steadman's complicity — too many people for the news not to have leaked out, too many people in the know for there not to have been an atmosphere he would have noticed at once.

That left the only other option — the rock ramparts of the canyon. Somewhere, somehow, there was a way out there. There had to be! All he had to do was find it.

In the next day or two — or more if need be — he would examine the rock face, every inch of it, on both sides of the canyon. Somewhere there had to be a fault, a trail up which the nimble-footed Texas Longhorns could be driven.

It was the small valleys that Jake had his mind on most of all. In one of them, somewhere, he expected to unmask the hidden trail and each one, as he came to it, he explored with extra thoroughness — until he came to the gulch of the Sweetwater creek.

Though open enough for anyone at its entrance to see almost the whole gulch, it was wide and went deep into the mountain. Here one could see cattle and buildings. It was the place of a homesteader, a small farmer whom Matt Steadman had permitted to make his living in the Palo Verde canyon, though he was not part of the Lazy Branch.

It was the only place on which the most obvious suspicion must rest. James Longlater had thought so. So had Matt Steadman, though he had no proof — not even the faintest factual grounds for suspicion. Just that they were there. And that homesteaders were often rustlers, too.

Matt Steadman had wanted to get them out. But Marshal Birch would not have it. And then the man had died, followed a short while after by his wife. So that now only the children were left — a girl now seventeen, and her fourteen-year-old brother. And they wouldn't budge — not even when Matt Steadman had doubled his offer for the place. Pigheadedness, he swore. They would starve. They couldn't cope.

That had been a year past now. They

were still there, still obstinate, still wouldn't move, still coping — though only just.

Texas Jake sat on his horse and surveyed the valley of the Sweetwater creek. His eyes went over the canyon walls inch by inch as far as he could see.

Nothing there. Nothing that he could see from this distance. And no place in the valley to hide even a single beast. Matt Steadman, if he wanted to, could sit his horse out there, exactly where Texas Jake was now sitting *his* horse, and count almost every beast in the little valley. And, anyway, he knew what they had, because he bought the odd excess beast or two from them at each round-up. It was an arrangement that suited both them and him.

Well, apparently there was nothing in the valley of the Sweetwater creek!

But Jake was not quite satisfied. He wanted to make sure, to be able to examine the rock wall at the far end of the little canyon from a closer distance.

He began to walk his horses into the valley.

Less than halfway in he found himself stopped at a mound of stones. A quiet voice spoke out of the stones.

'That's far enough, stranger!'

Jake looked up and found himself staring down the muzzle of an old hunting rifle. It was rock-steady, and the face squinting along the sights was young — very young.

'Put your hands on your saddle-horn,' said the young rifleman.

Texas Jake did just that.

'Who are you?' he said. 'Sarah or Mathew?'

'None of your damn business,' replied the young person promptly. 'Who are *you*?'

'Name's Jake. Folks call me Texas Jake. I want to talk to Sarah.'

'What about?'

'Cattle. Rustled cattle. From the Lazy B.'

The voice behind the rifle sharpened. 'We don't rustle cattle.'

'Didn't say you did,' said Jake. 'But I still want to talk to Sarah.'

'Well, you can't,' snapped the young rifleman. 'Now just turn round and get the hell out of here — before I put a slug through one o' them horses o' yourn.'

'Sure, sure,' said Texas Jake mildly. 'Just going, pardner.'

Gently he turned the horses and began to go back along the track he had come on.

He was frowning. He had seen two things that disturbed him. The first was an unusual shadow up the rock wall at the end of the valley that could, just possibly, be a cleft of some sort. The second was the briefest of glimpses of a figure in one of the barns that could, also just possibly, have been Ted Gonzales.

★ ★ ★

In the brief time that he had been in the Sweetwater gulch, Jake's sharp questing glances had picked up something else.

On the one side the ground sloped quite high up towards the rock wall. It was a slope of soil and scree and talus, with small trees and some bush, reaching right up to the cliff side. Except that Jake knew from experience that, whatever appearances might suggest, no vegetation usually went *right* up to a cliff wall. Especially not on scree like this.

There would be a gap between the trees and bushes and the cliff face, and along that gap there was likely to be a game trail, used by rabbits and other small game — a trail that could also be used by a man, and a trail that was high enough up the mountainside to make it possible to travel the whole length of the valley without being observed, especially if it were done at night.

There were several things that Jake wanted to know about the Sweetwater valley. The most important of them was that shadow up the rock face at the far end. Was that a possible trail out of the valley — or was it merely a shadow, an illusion?

The second thing Jake wanted to know was whether it had really been Ted Gonzales that he had caught a glimpse of and, if so, what was Ted doing there, given the determined hostility that he himself had encountered from the young rifleman? Did Ted have some arrangement with the two young people? Or was his presence unknown to them, and for a much more sinister purpose?

In all events, there was nothing that Jake could do about the Sweetwater gulch until nightfall. Moonrise, he knew, was about an hour after the coming of darkness, and the moon was full, shining out of a clear star-bedecked sky. All that he had already observed on previous nights.

Travel on foot, even through trees and brush, on such a night should be almost as easy as in daylight. In any case, the skills of moving at night, with or without moonlight, was another of the valuable lessons Old Piute, the Indian, had taught him on their hunting expeditions all those years ago when he was still a boy.

Jake found himself a small stretch of greensward among the trees beneath the rock wall of the Palo Verde valley. There was seepage water there, too — enough for the horses. He hobbled them and left them free to graze. Hobbled, or even unhobbled, it was unlikely that they would wander far from the water and grass of the camp site, and the site was far enough away from the entrance to the Sweetwater gulch, and sufficiently concealed among the trees, not to be easily come upon by any casual wanderer. The cattle were out on the valley floor, and any riders would be there, too.

Feeling secure in his concealment, Jake prepared himself a meal as he watched the sun going down. Then he packed a small parcel of food to take with him. Water he would have to look for in Sweetwater gulch — or go without. He would have to lie up there all day and return the following night. Once again, that was something he had got used to in his hunting days, often lying so still for hours on end in the cold or the rain or the baking sun that the quarry that he was stalking had almost walked over him.

Not that he would have to do anything so hardy this time. There would be plenty of shade and concealment on the slopes at the upper end of the Sweetwater gulch. It would merely be a matter of waiting till nightfall and returning by moonlight.

With the sun now down, and darkness rapidly filling the air, Jake began to prepare for his trip. First, he removed his boots and put on the moccasins he always carried with him. His six-guns and shell-belt were already safely tucked away in his bed-roll. He would be travelling light, taking only his two knives, one at each hip.

By now darkness had fully descended.

Carefully Jake doused the embers of his little fire, making certain that every bit of glow was extinguished. Sitting before the doused fire, Jake allowed his eyes to accommodate the light — changing from bright firelight to making use of the very minute amounts of light present in any darkness.

Once the accommodation had been achieved, Jake began to practise his night-vision. It was another trick learned during his hunting days, and it had taken a while to learn. The secret was that you see better in the dark from the periphery of your vision than from looking directly at an object. Jake had learned it, and learned it well — so well that they said he was able to stalk through the darkness almost with the surety of a cat.

Eventually the moon rose, bathing the world in a pale light, almost a paler version of daylight. Swiftly Jake made his way through the trees towards the distant entrance of the Sweetwater valley.

Was he on the threshold of discovering the way the rustled cattle were spirited out of the Palo Verde? Or was that shadow he had seen on the valley wall nothing but just that — a mere shadow?

Well, tomorrow at sunrise he would know. He would be able to see from close-up. He would also, he hoped, be able to see what Ted Gonzales was up to in the Sweetwater — if it really *had* been Ted Gonzales!

With a steady pace Jake moved through the moonlight — speedily and silently. He was learning anew how to feel the ground through his moccasins — how to feel it in the fraction of a second before he placed his full weight on the foot. Once more it was the challenge of the hunt, the excitement of it.

4

Texas Jake anticipated no difficulty and no trouble in the exercise he was attempting. Everything should go smoothly. He should be at the top of the Sweetwater valley well before dawn.

Then it would be merely a matter of waiting for the daylight, and watching the details of that suspicious shadow on the rock face gradually emerge as the light grew stronger. For the shape of the rock face, he knew from experience, would vary and change from minute to minute as the angle of the light from the climbing sun altered.

That constant change should be enough for him to determine the details of the cleft — if indeed it was a cleft. He should be able to see if there was any sign of a trail. And if, at the top end of the cleft, there was a way over the rim on to the mesa.

Although he anticipated no trouble, nevertheless, as he moved through the moonlight, Jake's senses were at full alert. When you are a hunter, he had learned, nothing is unimportant. Everything means something. You must read your surroundings — like the reader of a book interprets the printed letters on the pages before him.

You must feel the air. It is moving. Almost always it is moving. Even if only a very little. From which direction is it coming? What sounds does it bring with it? Small sounds. Insignificant sounds. But what are they? What creatures are making them — and why?

Or is it only the trees, and the brush? And when the sounds change? When they stop? What is there? A snake? A cat? A man?

And not only sounds. What scents do you smell? More important, what animals are aware of *your* scent going ahead of you on the gentle, almost imperceptible wind?

Everything means something. Always. This was the learning of the old hunting times, drummed into the boy until it became automatic in him — until he knew every sound in the wild, knew when things were right, and when they were wrong.

That was why now, as he moved into the entrance of the Sweetwater gulch, Jake was aware that something was wrong. The night sounds had changed, suddenly, subtly.

Jake found a concealed position from which he could, nevertheless, have full vision of the gulch entrance. Carefully he lowered himself to a comfortable full-length position on the ground. That way he would get the best view of whatever or whoever it was — looking up at them against the stars and the moonlight.

Motionless, Jake waited. At long last, in the near distance, he heard the scuffing of a stone and then later the clink of a horseshoe on rock.

Jake put his ear to the ground, but the sounds were too vague and soft.

Not many animals, he guessed. One horse, possibly two. Cattle? One, maybe. Or a couple. Not more. Patiently he waited, scanning the moonlit scene.

Then, quite suddenly, he saw them. Two riders, and a steer ahead of them.

As the riders came into the gulch entrance they moved up on the steer and, with bunched ropes, hit it hard across the rump. The steer lept forward and began to run. It was a Longhorn, nimble on its feet, and it made good going.

For a while the riders watched it, making sure that it was on its way up the valley to join the other few cattle up there, then one of the horsemen moved over to where Jake lay concealed.

For a few moments Jake wondered if he had been seen, but his reason told him that was not possible. The man had some other purpose. He was carrying something. Stopping at the edge of the rocks where Jake lay, he swung his arm, and hurled the object over the rocks, where it fell with a clang of iron.

'Son-of-a-bitch,' snarled the other rider viciously. 'Want to wake the whole world?'

But there was no sound or movement from the buildings up the valley, and the two horsemen, still swearing quietly at each other, turned their horses and left the way they had come.

Texas Jake waited until the riders were well clear of the gulch — until he could hear the horses loping off in the distance — then he got up and went in search of the piece of iron.

He found it reasonably quickly and held it up in the moonlight. As he had surmised, it was a running iron. It had no doubt been used to alter the Lazy B brand on the steer which was even now joining the other animals further up the gulch.

Tomorrow, or the day after, that

steer — and the iron — would be conveniently 'found' in a search by the Lazy B outfit, and would serve to 'prove' Sarah and Mathew to be rustlers!

Well, he would have something to say about that!

He placed the iron back where he had found it, and began to make his way up the mountainside.

But the matter of the iron was still bothering him. Not only the crude crime itself, but the question of who exactly was behind it. For, in the moonlight, he had been able to recognize the two riders as the men who had been with Ted Gonzales the day before — when he had stopped Judith's trap on the old coach road to El Pueblo.

Ted Gonzales! He kept on coming up against Ted Gonzales! Sooner or later there was going to have to be a real show-down between the two of them. He smiled at the prospect, a slight smile, thin on his lips.

But, in the moonlight, there was no smile in his cold eyes.

★ ★ ★

The way along below the rock face turned out to be rather less free than Jake had hoped. True, there were portions where, as he had expected, small-animal trails made the going easy. But these sections tended to be short, and to be interspersed with thicker clumps of bush. The easiest going was through the occasional batch of small trees, where the ground underneath was relatively free of bushes.

Cowboy-fashion, Jake kept track of time by the progress of the Big Dipper on its nightly journey round the North Star — one full turn every twenty-four hours — and, although his journey along under the rock wall took longer than he had expected, he still arrived at the head of the valley some hours before dawn.

The night air was cold, and Jake,

in the interests of travelling light, was wearing only his wool shirt and vest. At least, he reflected grimly, here in the canyon one was spared the constant, monotonous wind found on the plains and in the desert.

Jake was no stranger to discomfort. In his time he had endured ice and snow, hailstones that could stun a man, and lightning that killed many a plains rider. He could even lie motionless in heat that would fry an egg — or half immersed in numbingly cold water.

It was all, he had found, a matter of concentrating the mind, of sundering the emotions from the pain and discomfort of the body. It was the kind of concentration he had witnessed one day when he had seen an Indian pull an arrow from his own body without the slightest change of facial expression.

There was nothing Jake could do until daylight. Concentrating his mind to ignore the cold, he made a comfortable bed of soft brush, and went to sleep.

Yet, even while he slept, his senses were alert for anything unusual, any change in the pattern of the small night sounds on the hillside about him.

It was not a restful sleep. The old dream came back again, as it so often did. And, when at last he awoke, it was with all the bad memories once more fresh in his mind — memories of the first time that he had killed a man. And quite unnecessarily at that.

It was the occasion that, in the eyes of the public, had made him a gunman, and spread his reputation as a killer.

He had just reached the age of seventeen and, for the first time, had strapped on a gun-belt. Swaggering with a sense of new importance, he had not bothered to think through the full implications of his action — the fact that if you wore a gun you were going to have to use it.

Almost immediately he did have to use it.

He was in the saloon one day, drinking a glass of beer and feeling very grown-up and manly with this new toy of his. At the next table a handsome young woman, a saloon belle, bored with the man she was with, attempted to attract Jake's attention.

This infuriated her companion. Lurching up out of his seat, he flung his drink in Jake's face and snarled at him.

'You're wearing a gun, kid. Let's see if you can use it!'

With that he backed off and assumed the crouching stance of a man ready to draw. Immediately the people round about scattered. The girl tried to stop him, but he flung her aside.

'Fill your hand, kid. Let's see what sort of a man you are!'

Jake had been 'called'.

Stupid as the whole situation was, he had no option. He could not back down. That was unthinkable. He must make his play!

Slowly and deliberately he stood up.

But the slowness and the deliberation were nothing but a charade. He felt anything but deliberate. However, it gave him time to think.

Clumsily he got himself into a position to draw. He hoped that all those practice draws that he had done at home would see him through now.

In fact, it turned out that his reactions were reasonably quick and accurate. Automatically, the moment he saw the other man's hand move, he drew and fired once.

But he was late. By the time he pulled the trigger his opponent had already fired.

Fired — but missed.

Jake's bullet got him full in the chest.

But, in the split second between the other man's shot and his own, Jake realized that he need not have shot. His opponent would not have shot again. That was clear from his pose. There was no need to have killed him.

But he had. And that single action would remain with him to continue to plague his conscience. Not that

80

he appreciated that at the time. His feelings were a mixture partly of guilt, but mainly of relief that the other bullet had missed him.

It was Old Budge — no slouch with a six-gun himself — who had taken him aside afterwards and spelled out the full implications of his action.

'So you've killed your first man?'

Jake nodded, wondering what was coming next. The old cowhand's manner was not approving.

'Make you feel good, does it?'

Jake shook his head.

'It was a fair fight,' he added.

The older man nodded.

'Sure was. Between two idiots.'

He frowned at Jake.

'You're not bluffing yourself it was anything but a lucky accident that you even hit him?'

Jake said nothing.

'You were so ham-handed you would have been lucky to hit a whole barn — even at ten paces!'

His lip lifted scathingly.

'You're not a gunslinger's backside.'

Then he leaned forward and delivered his punch-line.

'That sure was the worst draw I ever saw. *But . . .* ' He paused dramatically. '*But* the story of this 'gunfight' is going to spread. It's going to grow. And you know what they're going to be saying?'

Again he paused, a glint of scorn in his eye.

'Greased lightning. That's what the story will be. Greased lightning. Your draw was so fast, they'll be saying, the other guy didn't even have a chance to get his gun fully out.'

This time his sneer was deliberate.

'Kid Jake they'll be calling you. Or some such rubbish. Kid Jake, the fastest gun in the West!'

He leaned back and regarded Jake gloomily.

'Every likkered-up cowhand west of the Mississippi is going to hear that story — and swear into his beer that he'll find you and beat you to the draw.'

He shook his head pityingly.

'From now on you're going to be killing one drunken fool after another.'

He looked down, and his next words were said quietly.

'Until someone kills *you*.'

He looked up, grim.

'*That's* what you have started for yourself today.'

There was no gainsaying the truth of Old Budge's words.

Jake looked back at the older man, his jaw set.

'So? What the hell am I supposed to do?'

'Two things,' snapped the old cowhand. 'First, you learn to shoot — properly.'

'And then?'

'Then you get the hell out of here. Go some place else — where nobody knows you.'

And, in the end, that's how it was.

It was Old Budge who taught Jake the finer points of gunslinging. Hour after hour he had him draw, using each hand in turn. And then both hands together. Day after day, hour after hour, it was draw, draw, draw — until he was as near greased lightning as any man could get.

And accurate.

So accurate that he could hit a smaller object at a longer distance than even Old Budge — and he could do that eight or nine shots out of ten consistently.

At that point Old Budge let him go — but with a warning.

'Don't rest on it,' he insisted. 'If you do you'll lose it. Practice, that's what you need. Hard practice — every day.'

Then he looked hard at Jake.

'And that killing. Forget it. You didn't have to kill him but you did. Now forget it.'

And Jake had tried to do that. But he couldn't. In his dreams at night it kept on coming back. Again and again.

★ ★ ★

The morning came at last, cold and clear.

Jake lay awake in that first light, stiff, half frozen. Carefully he began to move his limbs, getting some life into them, getting the blood to flow. Then he undid the small portion of packed food he had brought with him, and ate slowly. That, too, would put warmth into his stiff muscles.

Water he saw nowhere in the area about him. His thirst, not yet great, would have to wait until later — though, once the heat of the day came, water would become a necessity.

But now his attention was on two things. First, that shadow running up the cliff face. Eagerly he scanned it now in the changing light before sunrise. It was still some distance away from him. But it *was* a cleft in the rock. Of that he was now certain.

But how much of a cleft? How narrow? How steep? A Texas Longhorn was a nimble beast, almost goat-like in its ability to go virtually anywhere. But there were limits to the kind of gorge it could be driven up.

And what was at the top of the gorge? That, from where he now was, he could not see. But he knew from experience that gorges had a habit of looking an easy way up when seen from the bottom, only to end in enough of a precipice at the top to prevent access to the tableland above.

He would have to get nearer — probably even climb some way up the cleft in order to be certain one way or the other.

But could he get to the cleft? Now, in daylight? And without being seen from the house? He began to study the terrain carefully, particularly in relation to the farmhouse in the valley below.

And that was the second thing his attention had been on, right from the start: the farmhouse. It had taken him a while to realize why. The reason was that there was no movement, no sign of human life. And that was wrong.

True, it was not even sunrise yet. But a farmer's day began early. There should have been smoke coming from the chimney, the clatter of pots and pans, or milk pails. Something. Anything except the present dead silence.

Jake frowned. There was definitely something wrong there. Was it something to do with Ted Gonzales? Was it, in fact, really Ted Gonzales that he had seen there? He could not be sure. Anyway, there was nothing he could do about the farmhouse at the moment. The first priority was the cleft in the rockface.

The cover beween where he was and where the cleft began was not good. He would have to chance it, and just hope that he was not spotted from the farm buildings. And the sooner he got going the better his chances of avoiding being sighted. Turning on to his belly, he began to slide across the open patch of ground ahead of him.

In the end it took him at least an

hour to reach the bottom of the little gorge — an hour of careful, sometimes slow progress, often on his belly in the open, and always with a watchful eye on the farm buildings below for any sign that he may have been seen.

But there was nothing. Not the slightest evidence of human life from any of the small wooden buildings. Jake breathed a sigh of relief, though there was a troubled frown that went with the sigh. What the hell was going on down there?

The cleft, after all, turned out to be too narrow and too steep, full of smooth rockfaces and piles of small stones, and getting steeper the higher it went. No rustled cattle had gone out that way, that was for sure. And that made Sweetwater gulch simply another indentation into the rock wall surrounding the Palo Verde canyon that could now be eliminated in Jake's search for the route used by the rustlers.

Jake looked about him for a

comfortable site, well hidden from the valley below, where he would be able to spend the day until it was safe, at nightfall, to make his way back out of the little valley.

The site he selected had enough bush and small-tree cover to shield him from the now-risen sun and its heat, which was already beginning to build up. It was a place which had the additional advantage of a meagre but steady water-drip from the rock face.

Jake drank gratefully, patiently, one drip at a time. So intent was he on slaking his thirst that he failed to keep watch on the farm buildings below — until, more or less by accident, he did glance down into the valley.

What he saw there startled him into immediate concentration. Ted Gonzales had emerged from the farm house. With him were seventeen-year-old Sarah and her fourteen-year-old brother Mathew.

Both had their hands tied behind their backs, with a line leading back to Ted Gonzales — a line which Ted was even now making fast to one of the two trees that grew by the farm buildings.

Jake watched grimly as the big Mexican made his way to the other tree.

He moved round the trunk, looking up into the branches. When he found a branch apparently straight enough and strong enough for his purpose, he uncoiled the two lariats he carried over his arm, and threw the ends over the branch, so that each noose hung just head-height above the ground.

Ted Gonzales was about to hang the two young people!

The fury that rose up inside Jake he found hard to contain. Swiftly he cast his eye over the terrain leading down into the valley. Carefully he selected a route with the best available cover.

Then — quietly, deliberately, and in cold fury — he began to run.

5

The first part of the way down the hillside lay through trees. These, though somewhat sparse, provided cover adequate enough for a quietly running man.

But the trees soon gave way to brush, and here Jake had to make a swift decision. Straight ahead, in a direct line to the farm house, would land him, further down, into a short piece of open country before he reached the little wooden buildings.

Going that way — though it was the quickest — would mean that he would have to rely on Ted Gonzales having his back to him long enough for Jake to cover that open space. And that he had no means of guaranteeing.

The alternative was an oblique route, bending away well back of the farm buildings. This way he would be covered for almost the whole of his journey by a slight rise, and the dry bed of the stream along which he would be moving.

The trouble was that this route would take that much longer. Did he have the time?

It was a hard choice — a dangerous one for the young prisoners of Ted Gonzales. Go straight and Jake could well be caught in the open. And that would be that. Ted was wearing his six-gun. He also, surely, had a rifle somewhere in the background. Jake had nothing except his two knives.

His only hope was to get close to Ted before he was spotted. Everything depended on the element of surprise.

Reluctantly, Jake decided on the longer route — and set off, pacing himself deliberately.

That was another disadvantage of this longer way. He would have to travel more slowly. No point in arriving to confront Ted Gonzales in a state of panting exhaustion.

In the event, by the time he did reach the end of the route and came up behind the farm buildings out of Ted's sight, Jake felt that he had been running for hours.

Two things were worrying him. Was he, after all, too late? The sound of Ted's snarling voice, and the angry responses of both the young people, reassured Jake on that point.

The second matter for concern was could Ted possibly have an accomplice who had not yet shown himself? Jake did not think so. Any of Ted's thugs, if they had happened to be there, would surely not be sitting around inside the buildings. They would be outside with Ted, enjoying the fun.

At least Jake hoped so.

As Jake came up to the scene, moving swiftly from one small building to another, it was Sarah who saw him first.

This was the real moment of danger. What would she do — inadvertently, perhaps? Jake was still too far away.

In the event, the seventeen-year-old girl did not move a muscle. Nor by the slightest eye movement did she betray the presence of their potential rescuer.

Quite the contrary, in fact. At one point, when Ted was about to turn in Jake's direction, she kept his attention focussed on her by an angry tirade.

But what she said was apparently the last straw for the Mexican. The two lariats were already over the tree branch, their open nooses head-high above the ground.

Angrily Ted pushed the girl towards the first of the nooses. But she fought back strongly, and it took all the big man's strength to get her under the rope.

Now was the time for Jake to act. He could not risk further delay. Already the first of his heavy hunting-knives was out of its sheath and in his hand. One swift throw and it would bury its long razor-sharp blade deep between Ted's shoulders. Jake was as adept with a knife as with his six-guns.

But he hesitated. To kill a man by stabbing him in the back — even in these circumstances?

He couldn't do it.

Instead, Jake opted for a riskier action. His arm came up and the heavy knife curved through the air — to strike Ted Gonzales on the back of the head.

But not with its point — with the top of its haft.

It was a blow that momentarily stunned the big man. Before he could recover, Jake had leapt across the intervening yards and completed the job with two hard rabbit-punches to the neck.

Slowly Ted Gonzales crumpled to the ground. In a trice Jake had Ted's six-gun out of its holster, and was searching him for knives. He found five all told, one of them in his boot.

It took only a minute or two to untie the girl and, while she freed her brother, to use the rope to tie Ted's hands and feet.

Up till then not a word had been spoken. It was Sarah who uttered the first words, phlegmatic, matter-of-fact words.

'We sure are grateful to you, mister. Ted was dead-set on stringing us up this time.'

She had no time to say more because her brother had raised his arm and was pointing.

Jake turned to look.

Up the valley, coming towards them, riding fast, was a posse of men.

In the front rode the squat moustachioed figure of Marshal Jim Birch.

★ ★ ★

Sitting slumped in his saddle, Jim Birch was trying to work out what had happened.

Before him, hands tied, stood the large glowering figure of Ted Gonzales, casting nervous glances in the direction of the rest of the posse.

From them was coming a rising

murmur of anger directed towards the big Mexican. There were calls to string him up.

The two lariats still hung over the branch of the tree. It would take no more than a few concerted shoves and pushes to get him under one.

The man was beginning to sweat with fear.

The marshal appeared to be taking no notice of the hubbub behind him. However, his horse seemed to be a little restive, moving this way and that until — apparently by accident — it faced back towards the posse.

Only then did the more observant of the riders become aware that the marshal's shotgun was lying not-so-casually across his lap.

Gradually the hubbub died down, and they waited to see what the marshal intended to do.

But Jim Birch was worried. There were things here that did not add up.

Texas Jake, for a start.

A gunslinger? Without his guns? And wearing moccasins?

He it was, apparently, who had witnessed the misbranded maverick driven into the gulch, and the running iron conveniently hidden. And it was he who, next day, at the crucial moment, had stopped Gonzales in his tracks and saved Sarah.

But what was he doing in the gulch in the first place?

And then Ted Gonzales.

What in Heaven's name did he expect to achieve with that stupid ploy with the maverick and the running iron? Persuade the world that Sarah and Mathew were rustlers, perhaps even that they were the outfit rustling Lazy B stock by the hundred?

Ted wasn't that stupid, surely?

In any case, why then try to hang the youngsters? To appropriate Sweetwater for himself? Did he imagine he would be able to get away with that? Or perhaps he hoped to persuade everybody that the hangings were the work of somebody else — say Texas Jake.

It all seemed to the marshal not only evil but crazy as well.

And perhaps the most crazily unexpected thing of all, was that he and the posse should be there at all!

What had happened was that a slight, neatly dressed Mexican had appeared in his office and calmly informed him that if he wanted to prevent a double murder, he had better get himself and a posse out to Sweetwater immediately.

Now Jim Birch knew Mexicans well. He was not blinkered by the usual prejudice against them.

Sure, there were lazy, stupid, treacherous Mexicans. There were also not a few whites for whom the same descriptions were appropriate.

But there were also Mexicans, Jim was well aware, just as honest, competent, courageous and hard-working as the best of their American counterparts. And this slight young man, who had so confidently walked into his office, was clearly one such.

It took Jim only a few brief questions to convince himself that the young man knew what he was talking about, and that the matter was serious — and urgent.

Wearily, Jim Birch gave a heavy sigh. All in all, there did not seem to be many answers to all the questions in this confusion. About the only real, practical, undeniable fact that stood out of the morass was the glowering, trembling figure of the large Mexican before him.

'I'm taking you in, Ted,' Jim announced. 'And this time you're going to *stay* locked up — until the circuit comes round to try your case. Attempted murder that will be.'

They had found Ted's horse. A couple of the posse got him on it, hands still tied, and Jim Birch took the reins.

Like that, with its prisoner, the posse finally left the Sweetwater gulch on its way back to El Pueblo.

★ ★ ★

It was Sarah, with a woman's practicality, who brought Texas Jake's attention back to the real world.

'You'll be wanting to eat, surely,' she said.

It was a statement rather than a question. She must have realized that he had probably been all night in the valley and, though she could have no idea why he should be there, it was likely that he had not eaten for some time.

Sarah did not wait for a response from Jake, but went into the small wooden house, and soon the mouth-watering odour of fried pancakes drifted on to the now rapidly warming morning air.

It was a simple meal and — no doubt in Jake's honour — a more generous one than the brother and sister would have enjoyed on their own. But they were clearly grateful for what Jake had done for them, though they made no further reference to the matter.

Jake, however, was curious. How had two such young people managed to cope on their own? They were both well-built and strong. Jake could see that. Also that, in temperament, they were unemotional, and could likely endure hunger and hardship better than most.

Their farming skills they would, of course, have picked up from their parents. But, even then, there must have been times when they needed assistance of some kind, surely?

'Sure,' said Sarah. 'We could always go to Marshal Birch. He helped us a lot. Like when Colonel Steadman wanted to throw us out. But then, Colonel Steadman has made some things easy for us, too. He buys food from us for some of his animals, and for the ranch house. And sometimes he lets us take a maverick or two if we think they're ours. No, we don't have much trouble with Colonel Steadman now — only with Ted. Though even

Ted has never tried to hang us before.'

'Why did he try that?' asked Jake, curious.

Sarah shrugged.

'He wants Sweetwater,' she said simply. 'He's tried all sorts of things to get us out.'

'Well,' said Jake, 'looks like he won't be trying anything now for a while.'

'Mebbe,' said Sarah, with an obvious lack of conviction.

'You don't believe Jim Birch will keep him locked up?'

'No,' said Sarah. 'He's tried it before.'

'And?'

'Colonel Steadman got him out. Ted's got some hold over Matt Steadman. I don't know what. But he has. Matt'll persuade Jim Birch to let him go. Couple of days and you'll see Ted around again.'

She looked up suddenly at Jake. He noticed for the first time the clear, level grey of her eyes, the well arched eyebrows, the full cheeks and full mouth and, below, the firm line of the strong chin.

He realized that seventeen she might be in years, but in character and life experience she was already a full woman.

'Like I said,' she repeated. 'Couple of days and Ted'll be around again. Only . . . ' She paused and looked down for a moment. 'Only he had better not come round here again. Not ever. Not unless he wants to get shot.'

She looked up again at Jake.

'You married?' she asked, with a sudden, touching simplicity.

'No,' said Jake.

She nodded slowly, as if it took some time to absorb his answer.

'You're not aiming to marry? I mean . . . ' She hesitated, and a faint blush spread on her cheeks. 'There's nobody you're . . . ' Again she stopped, this time from embarrassment.

'There's nobody,' said Jake, feeling

uncomfortable but not knowing how to stop her.

Then he added quickly, 'But I'm not intending to get married. Not yet awhile.'

She nodded slowly, accepting his rejection of her unspoken offer without ill-feeling.

And he in turn, though feeling sorry for her, understood fully the urge that had driven her almost to ask him.

It was not a physical urge, nor an emotional one, but just straight, plain economic necessity. The farm needed a man about the place — a full-grown strong man, to take charge for a seventeen-year-old girl and a fourteen-year-old youth.

Stuck away here on the farm in the little valley, she did not have an awful lot of choice in looking for a husband.

It was Mathew who spoke next.

Up to now the lad had not said a word, leaving all the talking to his sister. It was evident that she was the controlling force in the partnership, and that he regarded her more as a mother-figure than a sister.

Now he said simply to Jake, 'You wanted to talk about rustling.'

It was the voice that had been behind the old hunting rifle the day before — the voice that had turned Jake back from his first attempted exploration of the valley.

Jake nodded.

'Sure,' he said — and waited.

'Like I told you,' said the boy. 'We don't rustle.'

Again Jake nodded, still waiting. He had the feeling that, now that he had the boy's confidence, he was about to be told something important.

The boy looked at Jake steadily. He had the same clear, level grey eyes as his sister, the same well-arched eyebrows and strong chin, the same air of strength and confidence. Another two, three years and he would be a full-grown man — a big one, and strong.

'It's full moon these nights,' he said at last.

Sudden comprehension dawned on Jake.

'That when they do the rustling — at full moon?'

Mathew nodded.

'Every full moon,' he said. 'I've watched them. From the mouth of the gulch. They round up the cattle, drive them up thataway.'

He gestured up towards the narrow end of the Palo Verde canyon — the direction from which Jake had come.

'And then?' said Jake. 'How do they get the cattle out of the canyon?'

Mathew shook his head.

'That's all I've seen,' he said.

'But it must be somewhere in that direction?'

The boy nodded.

'Must be,' he said. 'That's the way they always go.'

'Did you see who's doing it?'

Mathew shook his head.

'Too far away. Can't see faces that

far away. Specially not by moonlight.'

He was still holding something back, Jake felt.

'Did you tell Colonel Steadman what you saw?'

Mathew hesitated.

'The first time,' he said. 'Only the first time.'

'That's when Ted started harassing us,' said Sarah. 'Straight after we told Matt Steadman.'

'You reckon Ted's involved?'

She gave Jake a long steady look.

'That's how it looks,' she said. 'That's another reason for him trying to kill us — the main one, most likely.'

★ ★ ★

Jim Birch and the posse reached El Pueblo with their prisoner, tired and dusty after the long ride.

In the face of the marshal's firm determination, the posse had reluctantly abandoned the idea of lynching Ted

Gonzales, and now, grumbling and disgruntled, each peeled off home.

Jim sent Ted's horse, with one of them, down to the livery stable. Another he persuaded to drop into Pablo's café, to tell him to send over a meal for Jim and the prisoner. After that, he untied Ted's hands and locked him in the cell.

But things weren't over yet. Jim Birch knew that.

In a sense they were only just beginning. The climax was due to happen at any moment.

Jim sank back in his office chair, put his feet on the desk, pushed his hat over his eyes — and waited.

He did not have long to wait.

In less than thirty minutes there was the sound of a horse at the hitching rail outside his office, and a couple of minutes later the office door burst open and the rider strode in.

Jim pushed his hat to the back of his head.

'Sit down, Matt,' he said. 'I've been expecting you.'

Slowly, deliberately, his face grim and determined, Matt Steadman seated himself across the desk from the marshal. He looked really tired, haggard with exhaustion. In the dust-streaked pallor of his face, his eyes glowed with a burning, frenetic desperation. His voice, when he at last spoke, was hoarse and rasping.

'You know why I have come, Jim,' he said grimly, clamping shut his lips and pushing out his jaw determinedly. 'I don't have to spell it out for you.'

Slowly Jim nodded his head.

'Sure, Matt. I know. You want Ted. But you can't have him.'

Matt's eyes glowed more desperately. His voice was harsher.

'No? Why not? You've let him out into my care before, haven't you? And have I let you down when you did that?'

'No, Matt. Can't say you did.'

'Well, then? Why not this time?'

'This time's different.'

'How?'

Jim Birch slowly stroked his moustache.

'Them other times,' he said at last, slowly, 'well, they was for minor matters, mostly. Sorta minor, if you get my meaning. Fighting, breach of the peace, such like. And when he did kill someone, he always had witnesses to swear on the heads of their sainted and respected mothers that it had been a fair fight — or the other man drew first.'

Again Jim Birch fingered his moustache.

'At your insistence, Matt, I always gave Ted the benefit of the doubt. You always promised to keep him outta trouble — and, by and large, you did do that. It was the easiest way for me to handle things — short of running Ted outta town.'

He frowned and looked across the desk at the drawn face of the cattleman.

'But this time,' he said grimly, 'Ted's gone too far. I'm charging him with attempted murder.'

'Attempted murder!' snarled Matt, banging his fist on the desk. 'You must be mad!'

'There were ropes on that tree, Matt,' snapped the marshal. 'No two ways about that. There were ropes, two of them, 'ready noosed. He was going to hang those two, Matt! You can't persuade me he wasn't!'

'Hang them?' snorted Matt. 'Are you crazy? What would he want to do that for?'

Jim shrugged.

'Blame someone else, mebbe. Like Texas Jake. To get rid of him.'

'Rubbish!' snarled the cattleman. 'Absolute rubbish!'

The marshal said nothing for a few moments. Then he brought his feet down off the desk.

'What, then? Just playing games, was he?'

'Of course,' snapped Matt. 'You know Ted's jokes. Pretty gruesome, most of them. Those kids had been stealing cattle. Oh, nothing serious. The odd beast now and then. Ted wanted to scare the daylights out of them, that's all.'

Slowly the marshal shook his head.

'I've swallowed some queer excuses in my time,' he said. 'Mostly about Ted. And mostly thought up by you, Matt. But this time he went too far. He warn't playing no games with them two, Matt. He were serious, dead serious.'

Jim Birch stood up and stretched himself.

'I'm holding Ted, Matt, for when the circuit comes round. Like I said, the charge will be attempted murder.'

Matt, too, had stood up. In his haggard face his eyes burned even more fiercely. His jaw was clenched, and his lips were a thin line. In his hand he held a small pistol — a card-player's weapon. It was pointed directly at the marshal.

'Release him, Jim! Release him *now*!'

His voice was a soft, vehement hiss. The pistol moved slightly.

'I'm not playing games, Jim. I'd hate to kill you. But, by God, I'll do it — and right now — if you don't release Ted.'

Jim Birch was shaking his head sadly.

'And if I do release him, Matt? What then?'

'Then,' hissed Matt, 'we collect his horse and we — all three of us, because you are coming along, too — make for the Palo Verde.'

He leaned forward and tapped the fingers of his other hand on the marshal's desk.

'And don't let anybody try to stop us — or follow us, Jim. If you want to live, that is.'

6

Mathew lent Jake one of the farm's two horses, and himself rode out with Jake on the other one to bring it back from Jake's campsite.

The boy was uneasy, once outside the protection of Sweetwater. Jake could see that, and dismounted some way before the campsite.

'I'll walk the rest,' he said, handing the reins to Mathew.

The lad made no objection, merely nodding. However, as he turned the horses back towards the canyon, he hesitated, then spoke awkwardly.

'Sarah says to tell you you're welcome at Sweetwater. Any time. That goes for me, too. We 'ppreciate what you did. Anytime you need help we'll do what we can.'

'Good of you, pardner,' Jake grinned at him. 'And Sarah. Hope I won't need help. If I do, I'll sure remember your offer.'

Mathew gave an embarrassed nod, and kicked his mount into action.

For a while Jake stood and watched the boy and his two mounts on their way then, with a frown, he turned and concentrated on the task in hand. For Jake's decision not to ride all the way to his encampment was made not only because of Mathew's evident unease outside Sweetwater: it was also due to Jake's own natural caution.

The caution had been learned in his boyhood, in the woods, under the skilled tutelage of Old Piute. It was a caution which he had subsequently expanded and developed in his adult years until it had become an ingrained habit, one that had been responsible for saving his life on more than one occasion.

And now, Jake instinctively felt, was an occasion that required even more than his usual amount of caution.

He had not needed Judith's warning

that efforts would be made to kill him. That had, anyway, become more than clear on his two run-ins with Ted Gonzales. Also there was the fate of the previous agent that James Longlater had sent into the Palo Verde. Ted had hanged him, then had persuaded Matt Steadman the man had been an assassin.

So now, approaching the place where he had left his bed-roll and the two hobbled horses, Jake was in no mind to simply stroll in.

Instead he made a long detour, encircling the whole area quietly and with caution, his ears alert as ever for the normal sounds of nature, his nostrils constantly sniffing the shimmering, hardly moving air, his eyes everywhere, searching for the broken twig, the bruised leaf, the pressed suspicion of a foot's indentation among the grass tufts or on the moister ground.

Only when he had done a full half-circle around the site, at a distance, did he move in closer and repeat the process. That way, gradually, intently concentrating, he eventually arrived at the site.

Everything was as it should be. There was no hidden watcher. Nobody, as far as he could judge, had been at the site since he had left it the night before. The two hobbled horses were grazing peacefully. The sounds of nature, lazy in the heat, were normal in detail — just exactly what he would expect.

And yet . . . and yet . . . what was it? A sixth sense, perhaps? A hypersensitivity? What? Something was wrong. What, he didn't know. But something was not right! For a long time, motionless, half-hidden behind a young tree, Jake let his eyes rove over every detail of the campsite before him.

Somebody had been there — somebody who had taken the most minute care not to leave the slightest trace of his presence, and in that had failed by the merest fraction of an inch. Because

Jake, behind the tree, staring hard, could see that his bed-roll was not quite exactly as he had left it. It had been moved. Someone had moved it.

And they had not only moved it, as Jake found when eventually he opened it up. They had also taken both his six-guns, his Winchester, and his shell-belt. They had left him disarmed.

Jake's immediate reaction was to cast about him minutely for signs. He had seen none, but whoever had done this must have left some mark somewhere. Jake quartered the surrounding ground systematically, but it was only after some time, and at a little distance, that he picked up the first sign.

It was the mark of a portion of the side of a boot, imprinted in a small dampish patch of earth between rough grass tufts.

For a long few moments Jake studied the mark. It had not been made by his own boot. It was too small. But it was a rider's boot, in the conventional range rider's pattern — inward-sloping raised heel, pointed toe.

A rider's boot mark meant that a horse could not have been far away. No man walked farther wearing range rider's boots than he could help. It was too uncomfortable. So somewhere not too distant Jake was sure that he would find the marks of a horse.

Following the direction suggested by the partial boot print, Jake set out. He might even be in time to find not only the marks of the horse's hoofs but the horse itself — and the rider! And then? Without his guns what could he do? That, thought Jake grimly, he would decide if and when he came upon his quarry!

Cautiously but rapidly, quartering the ground ahead for further possible signs, Jake set out. But, at the back of his mind, a growing puzzlement was arising. Who had done this — and why? And why, furthermore, the elaborate efforts to conceal the fact that an intruder had been there at all? What was the purpose? Why disarm him?

The more he thought about the whole matter the more confusing he found the details. They just didn't add up — not in any way!

It was an uncertainty that would only succeed in adding to his caution.

* * *

It was the horse that Jake saw first. The animal stood in the dappled shade of a small wood of young trees under the canyon's rock wall. It stood quite motionless, the way horses do, drowsing in the baking heat, its head half down — dreaming of things that horses dream about.

As soon as he saw the horse, Jake immediately knew something about the rider. For the horse was a pinto, a piebald, and no range rider would be seen dead riding a pinto — not unless he was either an Indian or a Mexican *vaquero*. But the rider of this horse was no Indian. That was clear from the decorated forehead-band of the headstall on the animal, and from the long-skirted single-cinched Mexican saddle the horse had on.

So sharp was Jake's concentration on the saddled animal while he made these deductions that, for a few seconds, he failed to notice the rider himself a little distant from the horse.

He was a small man, the rider. Small but slim and neat in appearance. No dust-grimed sweating *vaquero* this — although his clothes were those of a Mexican range hand, and he wore the traditional Mexican shade-maker, the straw sombrero.

Like his horse, he was entirely motionless, sitting relaxed, cross-legged on a blanket in the shade. Before him, on the same blanket, lay Jake's weapons — the Winchester, the two six-guns, the shell-belt — which he seemed to be regarding with long concentration.

Jake was momentarily uncertain. What was the best thing to do? He was unarmed. His weapons had been taken by the stranger seated in the shade before him — and, in fact, lay there in full sight on the blanket. Yet there seemed nothing menacing in the attitude of the Mexican. And that was indeed puzzling. What was the man after? What did he want from Jake?

Jake's momentary hesitation was brought to an end by the rider himself. Lifting his head, he stared straight at the spot where Jake had concealed himself behind the trunk of a young tree, and spoke in a clear and precise voice.

'Señor Jake! Señor Texas Jake!'

He seemed to dwell on the words, as if they were almost amusing.

'You have come! At last! I expected you earlier, much earlier.'

His English had little trace of a Spanish accent. The words were comfortably spoken by one who was obviously quite at home in the language, though the care and precision of his enunciation betrayed the fact that this was not his home language. He seemed to be a well-educated man.

Not, Jake knew, that that in itself was particularly significant. Most range riders, cowboys or *vaqueros*, were of no, or very limited, education. Nevertheless, in their ranks could always be found the odd German count or French *marquis* or English milord — not to mention a sprinkling of Eastern school-teachers on occasion.

'My apologies,' said the stranger, 'for having taken the liberty of removing your weapons. My concern was that, on our first meeting, I should not be shot up — merely because of a misunderstanding.'

He stood up nimbly and strolled casually towards Jake — who was quick to note that the man was apparently unarmed. Half turning, the Mexican gestured back towards the weapons on the blanket.

'Your weapons are there. Please collect them — at your convenience.' He stopped and smiled slightly. 'Perhaps I should introduce myself. My name is Ramon Alvarez. I come from a small town across the border with the highly inflated name of Ciudad Conchita, 'Little Shell City' — which is entirely misleading, if I may say so.'

He paused briefly to chuckle, then went on. 'It is by no means big enough to be a city. In fact, it is of a size barely adequate to deserve the name of a small town. As for the *conchita* part of the name, the nearest shells are probably at the seacoast, very far away.'

He paused briefly again to bow ironically. 'Of this puffed-up self-important, over-large village, I, Ramon Alvarez, at your service, happen to be the principal (and only) law officer. What you, this side of the border, usually refer to as a marshal.'

His slight smile widened into a full grin, showing flashing white teeth beneath an aquiline nose in a dark-brown face.

'We have, I may add, you and I, a mutual acquaintance. Or should I say common enemy? One Ted Gonzales by name.'

He was still chuckling merrily at the thought of their mutual hostility to Ted when Jake emerged from behind the tree, and the Mexican, with a polite gesture of invitation, led him back to the blanket where his weapons lay.

★ ★ ★

It was a strange story that Ramon Alvarez had to tell — an extraordinary, dramatic tale of a sequence of events not many years old, but barely credible in the audacity and the scale of what had been done and was still being carried out.

It had all begun, as far as Ramon could find out, as ordinary straight-forward rustling — Arizona cows driven down across the border and finding willing buyers, with no questions asked.

Then suddenly two developments had taken place. The first was that the scale of rustling had increased substantially. Whole herds were being brought across the border — so much so that the Mexican authorities, not unwilling to turn a blind eye to the reasonable theft of gringo cattle (hadn't the gringos, after all, stolen all that territory from Mexico?) were becoming seriously embarrassed — and increasingly unable to think up reasonable excuses to meet the rising tide of irate Arizonan protests.

The second development was even more serious. Over a wide area, with *Ciudad Conchita* roughly at its centre, rich haciendas were being regularly looted, the inhabitants sometimes killed by the robbers, or abducted for ransom. Consignments of stolen treasure — gold, silver, diamonds and other precious stones, as well as silks and materials and works of art and other treasures, were being carted over the border.

It had only been recently established, explained Ramon, that the two developments were being run by one and the same gang. The gang brought the rustled cattle down into Mexico, robbed a hacienda or two, and escaped back over the border into the Arizona territory, from where the stolen treasure would be routed to dealers on the United States east coast.

'And you reckon,' said Jake, 'that it is Ted Gonzales who is responsible for all this?'

Ramon shook his head. 'Ted is a front man. Ted couldn't organize an operation as complicated as this. No, there's someone else behind Ted — someone with brains and organizing ability.' He grinned suddenly. 'Who is he? That's what I'm here to find out. *And* to take Ted back to *Ciudad Conchita* to face trial — but not yet. Not until he has led me to the man hiding behind him.'

For a moment Ramon looked thoughtful. 'Ted knows I'm here. And why. So he will kill me if he can. Only I have always been one step ahead of him — so far. That's because I have a pair of eyes and ears in Ted's camp — eyes and ears that warn me of his intentions.'

He suddenly looked up sharply at Jake.

'However,' he said grimly, 'that's not something that I can expect to last for ever. Sooner or later Ted is going to suspect that I am getting information. Then *he* is going to be one step ahead.' He looked thoughtful again. 'When *that* happens I don't expect to be able to continue avoiding him for long. Either he'll kill me, or I'll . . . ' He grinned and shook his head. 'The trouble is that I'm not much of a shot, and Ted is — what's the phrase? — greased lightning.'

The thought seemed to amuse him in a sort of self-derisive way.

'I'll have to make a plan of some kind — if I can think one up in time.'

And he laughed, shaking his head as if he did not really have all that much confidence in his ability to think up something in time. Then suddenly he became serious. 'But first, before anything else, I must show you the route by which the rustled cattle are taken out.'

★ ★ ★

The place was called Stony Rock Valley. One look at it and you could see why. It was a narrow, easily sloping gulch, leading up to the low precipice that prevented further progress to the mesa above.

Of all the indentations into the rock wall of the canyon that Jake had explored, this one had struck him at the time as the most barren of both soil and vegetation, being almost entirely flat rock.

For that very reason it had also seemed to Jake the most suitable, and therefore the most likely route by which the rustled stock were taken out of the Palo Verde canyon. You could drive a whole herd of cattle up Stony Rock Valley and leave hardly a trace of their passing.

So it was with considerable optimism

at the time that Jake had ridden up to the top of the little valley — right up to the rock wall that, low and broken-up though it was, however still turned out to be an insuperable barrier to any cattle, even the nimble-footed Texas Longhorn.

Disappointed at this finding, and still hoping against hope to discover some way by which the cattle could be got over this relatively low obstacle, Jake had carefully examined the rock wall — almost inch by inch. But no. In no way could cattle get past this obstacle. Reluctantly Jake had had to accept that fact.

And now, as he slouched comfortably in the saddle on the bigger of his two horses, and looked again up the gentle flat-rock incline of Stony Rock Valley, he remembered his fruitless search of the rock wall at the valley's top, and again shook his head with renewed disappointment.

A few yards away, relaxed on his pinto, Ramon grinned cheerfully.

'You don't think this is the place? Why not? It's ideal. What's more, it's the only possible way they can get the cattle out — without going past the ranch house and through the canyon entrance.'

Still shaking his head, Jake had to admit to himself that that was right — illogical though it seemed. If Mathew, observing the movements of the rustled cattle from the mouth of the Sweetwater, was correct in his conclusion that the exit for these cattle from the canyon *had* to be somewhere in the area that Jake and Ramon now were — *if* he was correct, then this had to be the place. There was no other gulch suitable.

But that still left the insuperable problem of the rock wall at the top of the little valley. How the hell did they manage to get the cattle past that?

It was not apparently a problem that seemed to worry Ramon in the slightest. He waved his hand airily.

'They must have some solution to

that. The rustlers, I mean. All we have to do is to wait and watch. They're going to move a herd one of these nights. Then we shall see how they do it. Until then . . . '

Again he waved an airy hand, and chuckled.

'The point is,' he added, with what Jake thought a rather strange logic, 'we *know* this is the place, rock wall at the top or no rock wall. We are certain. This *must* be the place. Therefore we can leave it to them to solve the problem of the rock wall at the top.'

He grinned happily at this masterly solution and Jake, still puzzled, had to admit to himself that there was really not very much else the two of them could do — except indeed to wait and see how, in fact, the rustlers solved the problem of the rock wall at the top of the little valley.

What neither Jake nor Ramon was aware of, as they sat their horses and gazed up the Stony Rock Valley, was that they were being closely observed from the rim of the very rock wall at the top of the valley that they were so concerned about.

Two men lay there, flat on their bellies, watching them intently.

One was a big man, with heavy sombre eyes and a thick black beard.

'They're on to us,' he muttered. 'You can see that by the way they're carrying on. They're on to us. They know this is the route we use.'

His companion, a runty little individual of indeterminate age, with a mouth twisted by an old injury, and a sparse, ragged moustache, bared a few tobacco-stained fangs in amusement.

'Mebbe,' he said, relaxed. 'But it don't matter. Not a son-of-a-bitch. 'Cause they still don't know how we do it. And that's what counts.'

'You goddam idiot son-of-a-bitch,' snarled the other, suddenly infuriated by the smaller man's complacency. 'They'll goddam find out, won't they? They'll bloody wait and see — *then* they'll know.'

He stared down at the two horsemen below.

'Get a message to Ted,' he said quietly. 'Urgent.'

The small man looked surprised.

'To gulch 'em?'

That brought the snarl back to his companion.

'That's right,' he snapped. 'Get rid of them. Eliminate them. Urgent. Now. I want them two dead as rattlers afore we move the cows.'

7

The cow was stuck deep in the mud, almost up to its neck. Its eyes, wide with fright, swivelled wildly, and every few seconds it issued a deep, plaintive moo.

Happy Harry brought his horse to a stop and unhitched his rope.

'It's too deep in,' said Hank, shaking his head. 'Won't never come out that easy.'

Automatic in the long-practised movements, Happy Harry made a large loop in the rope, dropping the honda about eighteen inches below his grip, swung the rope once, and let it go. It sailed through the air, opening wide as it went, and dropped neatly across the cow's horns. Happy Harry pulled it tight, dollied it round the saddle-horn, turned his horse and urged it forward. But the cow did not budge; as Hank had said, it was in too deep.

'Got its forelegs splayed out in front,' said Hank. 'Like a damn anchor.' As an ex-seaman he knew all about anchors.

Happy Harry nodded. 'Stupid son-of-a-bitch,' he growled.

Hank was already dismounting. 'We'll have to dig,' he said. 'Mud's soft enough. Keep that goddam rope tight. I don't want the son-of-a-bitch's horn in my guts.'

Harry chuckled. 'Couldn't do more harm than your rot-gut whiskey.'

But he made sure his well-schooled cow-pony kept a good tension on the rope.

Hank was already up to his thighs in the mud alongside the cow, groping down towards the hoof of the foreleg. As he had guessed, the leg was stretched out in front, anchoring the beast fast against any pull on Happy Harry's rope. Sweating, and cursing the stupidity of all bovine animals, Hank dug away in the soft mud with his hands, until he was able to bend the beast's foreleg back at the knee.

Taking a short length of twine from his pocket, Hank tied the hoof right up against the upper leg. Then, extricating himself with difficulty and much cursing from the mud, he moved round to the other side of the animal, to repeat the process. Eventually, that done, he again eased himself out of the clinging slime of the mud, and dropped the loop from his rope also over the cow's horns. With the two horses now putting their full weight on the ropes, the cow's plaintive protests bellowed out with renewed vigour.

'She'd better come this time,' growled Happy Harry, 'before we pull her stupid head off her stupid neck.'

Slowly and reluctantly the mud released its captive. As the beast emerged, Hank was again off his horse in time to remove his rope from the horns and hitch it round the animal's back legs. Like that, protesting but incapacitated, the cow was inspected by the men.

'Screw-worm,' said Harry. 'Like I thought.'

He pointed to the cuts and scratches on the animal where the maggots of the blowfly were writhing around. Cows often got themselves bogged down in the mud trying to get some relief from the irritation of the maggots.

Hank went back to his saddle-bags and returned with the standard screw-worm remedy — turpentine and tallow. They doctored the animal on one side, turned it over and did the other side too. Then, when Happy Harry had removed his rope from the cow's horns, and had remounted, Hank carefully and quickly released the thongs on the forelegs, and his rope from the hindlegs, and made a dash for his horse.

But the cow was in no fighting mood. It was too tired from its ordeal. Staggering to its feet, it stood awhile, then slowly began to make its way in the direction from which the sounds of the herd were coming. The two riders watched the animal. It had all been a routine chore, part of a cowhand's daily round. The cow would recover, but it would not go on the drive with the others.

It was on that coming drive that Happy Harry now had his mind. There was a lot about it to worry him.

★ ★ ★

Further down along the edge of the lake the cattle were being rounded up for the early morning start to the drive. Over three days the drive would take them to the round-up point where trail-boss Jim MacKenzie was collecting a herd for the long trek up to the northern railroads. There were to be some two hundred beeves from the Lazy B.

Hank shook his head at the meagre numbers. 'Used to be a lot more'n this afore the rustling started. Number gets smaller each time.'

Harry nodded gloomily. It was one of the things that was worrying him — had been for some time now. The way events were turning out there would soon be no more Lazy B — and no more work for him.

Hank was casting a cautious eye over the cattle so far collected. In the morning he would be one of the two point-riders — right up in front with the leader-steers, and in the full path of any stampede. He wanted no troublemakers in that herd, no stampede-starters! It did not take much to make cattle stampede, but there were some beasts who became so jittery that they had turned stampeding into a habit.

There was only one thing to do with such animals. If you couldn't keep them out of the trail-herd at the start, or sell them along the way, or use them as payment for traversing Indian territory or homesteaders' lands, you had to shoot them. You lost less cattle on the trail that way.

Over at the chuck wagon the cook was preparing the midday meal, watched with salivating interest by most of the off-duty cowhands, sitting around nearby on the grass.

He was a big dark fearsome man, the cook. Part Negro, part Indian, part who-knew-what, he did not take kindly to questions on the matter. Like all ranch cooks, he made sure he kept his clientele in continuous awe of him, each man afraid that the cook's displeasure might earn him the more meagre portions at a meal.

Happy Harry approached him with cheerful caution. 'What's it today, Cookie?'

The big man straightened himself up from his steaming pots, wiped a huge forearm over his sweating brow and gave an unusual grin.

'Son-of-a-bitch stew,' he announced triumphantly.

A rare delicacy! Harry could see why there was such anticipation among the waiting diners on the grass. The previous day a calf had broken its leg and had to be shot. The range hands were about to reap the benefit of that event, for in the stew were the calf's liver, kidneys and tongue, marrow-gut (the half digested contents of the tube connecting the ruminant's stomachs — put in for flavour), its brains, and whatever else this particular cook's recipe required. It was a traditional delicacy on the range.

Harry cast his eye over the chuck wagon. 'How do you like the new wagon?' he asked, and received an even bigger grin from the cook — who seemed to be in an unusually buoyant mood that day.

'Like it fine,' he said. 'Better'n the old son-of-a-bitch.'

The new wagon was the result of Colonel Steadman's ingenuity and experience. On to a prairie-schooner base he had added a large tank for fresh water on one side, balanced on the other by a heavy toolbox. In the narrow body of the wagon were kept guns and ammunition, wagon-sheets, and a spare wheel — plus the slickers and bed-rolls of the riders when they were on the trail.

But it was at the rear of the vehicle that Matt Steadman's genius had really shone through. For here was a large store-cupboard with shelves and pigeon-holes for all the cooking ingredients — all covered by a large hinged lid that opened down on to a strong supporting leg, and formed a working table for the cook. Compared to the primitive hardship of earlier chuck wagons this was a kitchen for de luxe cuisine!

Happy Harry chuckled at the cook's enthusiasm. He felt greatly relieved to know that when, in the pre-dawn hours of the next morning, he rode out as the trail-boss of this small herd of two hundred cattle, he would have a contented cook and a reasonably well-fed bunch of range hands.

As he rode off towards where the herd was being rounded up, he heard the cook's traditional stentorian bellow: 'Come and get it — afore I throw the lot into the lake!' His audience needed no urging.

★ ★ ★

Later, after a good helping of son-of-a-bitch stew, washed down by a couple of mugs of Arbuckle's coffee, Happy Harry's thoughts turned to the Sweetwater valley. The previous day, when Marshal Jim Birch had led his posse into Sweetwater and found Ted Gonzales about to hang its two young occupants, Harry had been tagging along to see what it was all about.

Harry had no liking for Ted Gonzales. Quite the contrary. But there had never been anything he could do about that. Ted's reputation, both with the six-gun and with the knife, made folks go warily in dealing with him. And Harry was no fool. With a six-gun he could put a cow out of its misery, or take a pot at a skulking coyote. But that was about all. He was far too sensible to fancy himself a gunfighter.

His rage, however, when he saw what Ted had been about to do in Sweetwater was so great that he would have been prepared to tackle the man with his bare hands. And if Ted had been lynched on the spot, Harry's would certainly have been one of the first pairs of hands on the rope. But Marshal Birch and his posse had taken Ted away, and Harry, too, had left the gulch with them.

In thinking about the incident afterwards, however, Harry had found to his surprise that it was not Ted Gonzales, or Ted's intended crime that occupied his thoughts, but the face and figure of the girl.

There had been strength there — a womanly strength beyond her years. He had been struck by her dignity and her poise, and the straight, level gaze of her grey eyes beneath those arched brows when she had looked at him — just once, briefly.

What had startled Harry about that look, brief though it was, was that it was no mere passing glance. She had really looked at him, right into his eyes, in a way that you look at somebody you want to get to know. They had not spoken, and she had not looked at him again. Yet Harry had the feeling that she was aware of his presence all the time he was there, and after he left Sweetwater he could not forget her. She kept coming back into his mind's eye, her face, her figure, the womanness of her. It was a feeling he had never experienced before.

He began to scheme and plot within himself as to how he could get to see her again. And only now, after the midday meal, had the idea come to him like a flash of inspiration. With a strange, unaccustomed excitement rising inside him, Happy Harry mounted his horse and set off for the Sweetwater gulch.

* * *

As he rode into Sweetwater, Happy Harry half expected that he would be challenged. That was, after all, only to be expected, given the events of yesterday. But there was no challenge. No doubt his arrival had been observed. It would be rash of them not to be aware of anybody entering their valley. He hoped that the reason there had been no challenge was because they had recognized him for what he was — a friend.

He was walking his horse, taking his time, looking about him, noting the lay of the land, the thickness of the grama grass — that wonderful fodder that, together with buffalo grass, had kept the buffalo alive in their millions all over the western plains until the firesticks of the red and white men began to wipe them out. The grama's secret was that it was an all-year crop, drying in the summer heat to a fine, brown, nutritious hay-on-the-root that the Texas Longhorns thrived on as much as the buffalo had.

There were sheep, he noticed. A small flock, sheared now of their wool. He wondered which of the two did the shearing. Both, probably. Though it was no doubt Sarah who spun and knitted or wove the resulting product. In the winter evenings, he supposed, when farm chores were mostly on a maintenance basis, and time hung heavy in the cold and in the longer hours of darkness.

Further ahead were the crops. Maize, a little wheat, barley, vegetables. And no doubt there were chickens somewhere. Behind the little wooden farmhouse, he presumed. Outside the farmhouse door Sarah stood, watching his progress until he reached her, dismounted, and dropped the reins over the head of his pony to ground-tie him.

'Good day, ma'am,' he said, touching his hat with an unusual gallantry.

'Sarah will do,' she said mildly without censure, and he immediately felt embarrassed in case she should think that he had been teasing her, calling her, a girl of seventeen, ma'am.

'You're Harry,' she said, her gaze upon him clear and straight. 'You were here yesterday.'

'I was,' he said, and frowned angrily at the memory of what had happened. 'It was a bad business.'

She gave the slightest of smiles. 'We survived,' she said simply. Clearly a young woman not easily fazed. Her smile widened. 'Will you have coffee, Harry?'

'Indeed, ma'am.'

'Sarah.'

'Sarah.'

She laughed and led him inside the little farmhouse.

'You're going on a drive tomorrow,' she said, as she prepared the coffee. 'When will you be back?'

'Four, five days most likely. That's what I called about, see.'

She looked at him, her arched eyebrows slightly raised, waiting.

'I thought you might be needing

things. Supplies, groceries.'

She turned back to the coffee. 'Needing's one thing,' she said flatly. 'Having the money to pay for it all is another.'

They talked a bit about the little farm, about her parents and her brother. Then, at last, he said he would be going. 'Make that list,' he said. 'What you need. I'll see what I can fix up. Payment can wait.'

She frowned. 'I'll not get into debt,' she said firmly. 'Not that.'

Harry shook his head. 'You won't,' he said. 'Trust me. Now make that list.'

She hesitated, but only for a moment. Then she went to the wardrobe that had been her mother's, found the stub of a pencil and, on the back of some wrapping paper, began slowly and carefully to form the letters and figures her mother had so painstakingly taught her during the long winter evenings, when she was still a child.

It was already dark when Harry got back to the camp. Out of a clear star-spangled sky the full moon shed its bright light into the cold night air. Around the chuck wagon, its boom already from habit pointing to the North Star to give the trail-boss his (in this case unneeded) direction in the morning, there was silence. It was the cook, after all, who would be first up in the pre-dawn hours, preparing the first meal of the day.

Round and about the chuck wagon, on the grass, tightly snug in their bed-rolls, slept the men who would be taking over the later two-hour night-shifts with the herd. For ease of mounting, and for convenience, some of them had their cow-ponies staked out near to them. It was less trouble than having to find them in the remuda — the horse pool looked after at this time of day by the junior rider acting as night-hawk.

Further out in the moonlit night the herd reclined, contentedly chewing the cud. They would stay like this, provided that nothing disturbed them, until around midnight when, for no known reason, they would all suddenly stand up, yawn, stretch, and then gradually sink back to a new position.

From the outskirts of the herd came the sound of the singing of the two riders circling the recumbent animals, one going round clockwise, the other counter-clockwise.

The songs were mournful dirges — old hymn tunes with new words, adapted sea-shanties, momentary improvisations.

The cattle liked the singing. It reassured them, and the more mournful the tune, the more restful they seemed to find it.

For the riders the singing, in or out of tune, served to locate each of the pair to the other — a precaution in case of any trouble with the herd.

Happy Harry found his bed-roll, off-saddled his horse and let it loose into the remuda. That done, he inserted himself gratefully into his bed and was immediately asleep.

Around him the riders were being woken for the new shift, each man's name being called quietly by his waker. Custom — and good sense — decreed that a sleeper was never shaken, or even touched. Such a waker could well get a bullet in reply!

8

Texas Jake was uneasy. It was an unease that had been growing ever since the moment that he and Ramon had left Stony Rock Valley. In the first place, *why* was Ramon so certain that there must be a way for the cattle through the rock wall at the top of the valley? Jake, after all, had examined that rock wall on a previous occasion — with considerable care. He had been sure then that there was no way past that barrier for cattle.

Yet Ramon was totally relaxed about the matter — saying merely that he knew this was the way the cattle were taken out, so there *must* be some way through that barrier. *How* did he know that? Presumably from his 'eyes and ears' in Ted Gonzales's camp. But how reliable were those 'eyes and ears'? Ramon seemed to have full confidence in the person concerned. Jake was less confident. Ramon was also totally relaxed about waiting for the rustlers to act.

'They'll wait for the trail-drive to be gone before they begin. You'll see. They've got to wait for that first. Then they'll get going. Pronto. The very next night, probably. All we've got to do is just sit around and wait.'

And that was just exactly what they had done. But not in their camp. Jake's unease had seen to that. Hidden away though they were, and probably safe enough except from anybody deliberately searching for them, nevertheless in that camp they were blind. From there they could not see what was going on in the valley. It was that which had made Jake uneasy.

Ramon was reluctant to move. However, eventually Jake talked him round, and they went, with the three horses, to find a new site. It took them all morning, among the trees on the slope below the rock face, before they found a place that satisfied Jake.

Once again it was a small dell, with a trickle of seepage water out of the cliff, giving just enough of a pool for the horses. There was enough grass there for fodder, and it was not easy for the hobbled mounts to stray, because of the enclosed nature of the dell. They cooked their meals down there, too — with absolutely no chance of any whiff of tell-tale smoke emerging above the trees. But, though they cooked and ate in the dell, they slept and spent the rest of the time a few yards higher up the slope, right under the rock face. Concealed there, the whole valley was open to their view. Not only the valley floor, but also the slope they were on, for miles on either side.

Once ensconced there, Jake felt a mite less uneasy. At least there they would have full warning of anything suspicious, anything possibly threatening. Nevertheless, he did not let that lull him into a false sense of security. While Ramon often pulled his sombrero over his eyes and dozed in the shade, Jake's eyes were constantly on the move, reading every possible sign, watching every bit of activity in the valley.

He watched Hank and Happy Harry pull the cow out of the mud and, further down the lake shore, saw another beast receiving the same rescuing service from another couple of range hands. Though unaware of the contents of the meal, he watched the riders at their midday repast, and saw Happy Harry ride off to Sweetwater valley.

It all looked so peaceful. Deceptively peaceful. Far *too* peaceful. Something was about to happen. Jake felt sure of that. Somehow, from long experience, he felt it in his bones.

★ ★ ★

But the hours passed and nothing happened. Perhaps, after all, he was wrong. Perhaps nothing *was* going to happen. Ramon was right. Nothing would happen. Not until tomorrow night. Not until the rustlers moved the cattle.

And, in fact, the night too passed peacefully enough. In the pre-dawn gloom Jake watched the cook down below at the chuck wagon prepare the morning meal, and then rouse the hands with his ever-repeated threat to throw it all away. He saw the night-hawk bring in the remuda of horses, holding them with a temporary rope-corral, and saw Happy Harry, as trail-boss, ride off to fix the first stopping place for the herd, followed not long after by the cook in his chuck wagon, whipping up his mule team, his mind on the meal he would be preparing as soon as Harry had picked his site.

And then he saw the herd, moving off, slowly at first, until the leader-steers pushed their way to the front and set the pace, guided by the two point men, the rest of the column being kept in column by the flank-riders, and the stragglers quirted forward by those riding drag, their faces already masked by their kerchiefs, although as yet in the early dew-soaked morning there was little dust to speak of. The trail-drive was on its way.

As the sun came up, Jake and Ramon went down into the dell to prepare their meal, returning soon after for Jake to continue his watch on the valley, and for Ramon to launch once more into one of his stories. He was a good story teller, in the tradition of the range, where men, of necessity, were accustomed to make their own entertainment. There were, after all, long periods in their otherwise busy lives when they had to sit or lie around just waiting. In winter particularly. Or between shifts on the range. Or sometimes evenings, over a fire of scraps of wood or buffalo chips. Then they would have songs. Or someone would play an instrument — a guitar, or a mouth-organ, or what was known as a Jew's harp.

Or maybe they would stage a mock hanging — with a kangaroo court, a bloodthirsty prosecutor, a hanging judge, and an accused guilty before the proceedings had even begun.

But now and again it would be just a story teller, though good story tellers were rarer than champagne. Stories would be about the past, strange events, strange people, hair-raising adventures, often personal experiences of the teller.

Ramon's stories, Jake discovered to his surprise, were different. They were about the past, but the real past. And not mere personal anecdotes, but what folks liked to call history. Ramon was keen on history. He had spent much time in libraries at monasteries and other such places in Mexico, looking up old records, perusing letters and documents, talking to old people who remembered some of those far-off happenings.

Jake learned how the Spanish had come to the continent, bringing horses and cattle. How they had set up mission stations in California a hundred and more years earlier, ranching cattle, not for their meat, but to sell the hides and tallow to Yankee trading schooners bound for the east-coast trade.

It was there, in California, that the first *vaqueros* were made — Indians, taught by the Spanish to ride, using a version of the old Spanish war saddle, with cantle and saddle-horn, and controlling the cattle with the Spanish rope they called *la reata*, the lariat. It was Spanish horses and Spanish cattle, escaping into the wild, that had begun the herds of wild mustangs and Texas Longhorns, and set the stage for the future Western cattle industry — not to mention giving the formerly horseless Plains Indians a valuable addition to their military strength.

For Texas Jake these stories of Ramon's opened up a fascinating new outlook on the past — a world that the Mexican, with his obvious enthusiasm for the subject, brought vividly to life.

It was during one of these stories that Texas Jake first saw the riders.

★ ★ ★

There were six of them. Tall lean men riding big strong horses. From the north they seemed to be, for their hats were all Montana Peaks, though that was not necessarily proof. Jake watched them, through the shimmering heat of the early morning, carefully quartering the hillside under the rock face, coming gradually towards him.

They worked steadily, thoroughly, in pairs. One lot going up in among the trees; another pair checking each draw; the third couple keeping watch, immobile, just watching, their rifles out of their scabbards and held across their saddles. It required no great feat of imagination to guess for whom they were looking! The question was: what to do? Jake frowned, and considered the matter.

Ramon's reaction was merely to

shrug. 'Ted's men,' he said, with a quick smile and a white flash of teeth. 'It's a show-down. We fight.'

He certainly did not lack courage, the small slim Mexican, Jake reflected. For Ramon must know, just as well as he, Jake, did that, against six such obviously experienced professional killers, the two of them did not stand a hope in hell. Two men they could have coped with. Three even. But six men, looking as dangerous as these, never. And they could not get away from them. Not without being noticed. Even if they moved carefully away, staying hidden by the trees, the six would eventually catch up with them. The trees did not last forever. There were open spaces to cross. And all the time the six would be closing in on them. It was a pretty hopeless situation. Unless . . .

Suddenly the idea came to Jake. A chance, but a slim one. If they could just reach Sweetwater! Mathew had said that he and Sarah could be called on should he, Jake, ever need them.

Jake had thanked him and thought no more about it. He could, at the time, envisage no situation where he would have to take advantage of the offer. But now it was different. Now it was a matter of life or death — nothing less. He and Ramon *must* reach Sweetwater. With four guns, instead of just two, they at least stood a better chance.

Quickly and briefly he explained to the Mexican. Another white flash of teeth in a quick smile, and they slipped quietly down to unhobble the horses.

★ ★ ★

The trouble with the slope of any mountainside anywhere is always that you are having to cross little gullies, streamlets, or dried-up small watercourses — all with slight humped ridges in between, and some even with perpendicular banks that, although not very high, are still an impediment to horses.

This particular slope below the rock

face of the canyon was no exception, and Jake and Ramon found it hard going. More important, it was also slow going. The six horsemen, despite the time consumed in their search, were still making better time than the two fugitives. It would not be long before they caught up! Sweetwater seemed an awful long way off! Jake and Ramon gritted their teeth and pushed on as fast as they could.

One difficulty they had was the need for silence. Sounds, some of them reflected from the nearby rock face, travelled far in the canyon. The clink of a horseshoe on stone, or the tumbling of a dislodged small boulder could be their undoing. Also, they had to remain under cover. Most of the way the tree cover was thick enough to hide them. But there were patches where the trees thinned out, and even short stretches completely bare of trees. When they came across such areas they had to spend valuable time going round them.

At last they came to a point where the tree cover gave out completely. Jake, screwing up his eyes against the sun, made a rapid calculation. Sweetwater was not far now, but the pursuers had caught up a lot on the two of them. Was the gap between pursuers and pursued still sufficient for Jake and Ramon to make it into Sweetwater in a straight race across the flat?

Jake thought so — just. But they would have to quirt the horses hard. Also, Jake hoped for the element of initial surprise in the pursuers, as the two of them broke cover, to gain them a minute-or-two's extra time before the six could collect themselves and start after them.

Briefly, Jake explained his thinking to Ramon and received Ramon's habitual flashing grin in return. There seemed to be not an atom of fear in the Mexican. He appeared to be able to take life as it came, to meet events head on, no matter how threatening they might seem. Jake grinned in return, heartened by the optimism of his partner. Putting their horses almost immediately into a gallop, the two emerged from the trees and, quirting hard, made for Sweetwater.

For the first minute or so, Jake could hardly believe their luck! It seemed that, as he had hoped, they had caught the others by surprise, and it must have been a full two minutes before they heard the first shouts from the two watching horsemen to their companions up among the trees.

That was another advantage Jake had reckoned on. The horsemen up on the slope, among the trees, would take a few minutes to get down on to the flat. In the chase, therefore, they would be way behind. The real threat to the fugitives would come only from the two men who had acted as watchers and who, therefore, pausing only to slip their rifles back into their scabbards, were able to set off immediately in pursuit.

★ ★ ★

The race was on. A race for the very lives of the two fugitives! There could be no doubt about that. There would be no quarter given by the six hunters. They were out to eliminate Jake and Ramon — nothing less. There was going to be no way to stop them except to kill them, all six of them. That was clear. But at the moment there was little chance of that. It would be all that Jake and Ramon could manage at this stage merely to save their own lives. The two fugitives bent low in their saddles and quirted their mounts.

But now the first unexpected hitch in their escape plan became apparent — one that Jake had not foreseen. The pinto was too slow! Though Ramon spurred and quirted it, the 'paint' just did not have it in him. The horse was doing its best. Jake could see that. The trouble was that its best was far from good enough, and the two riders leading the pursuit rapidly began to gain on the fugitives. And now, not far behind them, came the other four, lashing their horses unmercifully. They had to be slowed down — somehow!

In a trice, Jake had his six-gun out and, turning in the saddle, he loosed off a couple of rounds at the leading pair of riders. But it made not the slightest impression. They kept coming. They were effectively out of sidearms' range, and they were well aware of that. Shots from a six-gun they could safely ignore — for the time being. Grimly Jake holstered the weapon, and reached for the Winchester.

To get a rifle out of its scabbard on a galloping horse is a lot more inconvenient than it sounds, and by the time Jake had the Winchester out, and had swung round in the saddle with the rifle to his shoulder, the leading pair were almost near enough to be breathing down Jake's neck! But, with the rifle now in his hand, that was to Jake's advantage. The nearer the better!

He gave a mirthless grin, snuggled the butt of the weapon into his shoulder and took aim.

Shooting a rifle, while twisted round in the saddle of a madly galloping horse, and aiming at the crouching figure of a pursuing rider, also on a madly galloping horse, is not likely to produce a result of pin-point accuracy! Nevertheless, there is something that is possessed by only a natural marksman. Call it instinct. Call it balance. Call it judgement. Call it luck, even, if you like.

Whatever it is, it is a quality that can cause a moving marksman on a moving animal to come surprisingly close to hitting his target!

And Jake was a marksman — a first-class shot, a natural, even a relaxed performer, a man who had an instinct, a feel for his weapon — almost as if that weapon was part of his own body!

When he drew and fired his six-guns, one-or two-handed, Jake did not have to think about the draw, or about the target. It was all automatic, ingrained into him after all the hundreds of hours of practice. He shot by instinct, by feel. Similarly now with the Winchester. The first slug went past the head of the left-hand rider so close that it almost took his ear-lobe off.

The man jerked up in the saddle, startled, and the next shot took his hat off his head. Pulling hard on the reins, the man immediately dropped further back — and stayed there. His companion, however, had for the moment noticed none of this. He had heard the sounds of Jake's shots but, since they had come nowhere near him, he felt safe in ignoring them. A serious mistake on his part, which almost cost him his life. Jake's third shot not only took the hat off his head, it almost parted the hairs on his head!

For a moment the man swayed dangerously in the saddle, pulling his mount up and dropping back to where his companion had now been joined by two of the other riders. They had seen what had happened, and for a while they all kept, if not out of range, at least far enough back to make any shooting a lot less productive.

After all, they reckoned, they were not in all *that* much of a hurry. There was nowhere for the fugitives to hide, nowhere they could go. There was, in a word, no possibility of escape for them. Their elimination would now merely take a little longer, that was all.

★ ★ ★

Sweetwater — at last!

As he and Ramon galloped into the valley, Jake fully expected to hear the sounds of shots aimed at their pursuers. After all, Sarah and Mathew must have heard the earlier shooting. And, after their last experience with Ted Gonzales, they must surely be on guard against any further incursions into their little valley.

But, to Jake's alarm, as the two riders

galloped in past the entrance to the gulch, there were no shots — nothing to threaten the oncoming pursuers who, clearly, felt that they now had their quarry boxed up. The six slowed their horses down, waiting to see what Jake and Ramon now intended to do.

In fact, Jake, from his previous experience of the gulch, had already worked out a plan of strategy. Only his plan had envisaged four rifles, not a mere two!

Part of the way into the gulch there were two useful rocky outcrops, together with stone piles around them, one on each side of the valley, but still fairly near to each other. It was from one of these stone piles that Mathew had originally challenged Jake on his first foray into the gulch.

Jake signalled to Ramon to take one outcrop while he took the other. Dismounting fast, but seeing that their horses were safe behind the protection of the rocks, the two riders seized their rifles and found themselves protected firing positions among the rocks, facing back towards their pursuers.

The latter, noting that their quarry seemed at last intent on standing and fighting, dismounted at a safe distance, found their horses safe grazing, and hobbled them. That done, they took their rifles and fanned out, seeking whatever cover was available.

Jake set his jaw grimly. He knew only too well what the tactics of the six would now be — covering fire from two or three of them while the others crept forward to repeat the process. That way, it would not be too long before the two pairs on the flanks had worked their way around to attack Jake and Ramon from both sides. That, the two of them must do their best to stop at all costs! Each shot of their's must tell! If they could just eliminate even two of the attackers, that would give them at least a more even chance. But where, in God's name, were Sarah and Mathew? He had relied on their assistance.

A shot rang out. It was Ramon. But he seemed to have missed his target. Jake kept his eyes skinned for the slightest chance of a shot.

But the attackers were cautious — skilful in their concealment, and alarmingly rapid in their progress forward. Things were swiftly approaching the crunch.

Ah, well, Jake told himself grimly, they would not get him alive. And he would take as many of them with him as he could.

Just as he completed this dark pledge to himself, Jake was astounded to hear a veritable fusillade of shots.

Not from himself, or from Ramon.

And not from the attackers!

The shooting was coming from *behind* the attackers!

It must be Sarah and Mathew!

Obviously the young people had skilfully laid an ambush for the intruders — who were now in utter startled confusion.

Jake saw one man throw up his

hands and fall out from behind his rock cover to lie still in the open. Another, attempting to run to a new site of concealment, turned a half-somersault as a bullet struck him, and lay motionless where he fell.

A surprised head appeared above a rock right in the sights of Jake's rifle — and fell back with Jake's bullet through his brain.

Two more shots from Sarah and Mathew, plus a running figure that Jake dispatched before he had completed three strides: then silence.

Slowly, first Mathew from one side, then Sarah from the other, emerged into the open, their rifles at the ready.

But their caution proved unnecessary.

As Jake and Ramon, too, emerged from their concealment, it was clear that all six killers were dead.

9

On his horse, in the moonlight, Ted Gonzales sat very still, listening. From the near distance, quite distinctly, came the unmistakable sound of cattle moving forward. Ted glanced briefly up at the sky, and scowled. It was getting late. Soon, above the sound of the moving cattle, came the sharper clip-clop of a horse, and one of the hands rode up.

'All there, boss,' he said laconically.

'How many?' snapped Ted, still scowling.

'Many's we could find. Hundred, hundred-fifty. We didn't count.'

Ted shook his head irritably. 'They count there.' He pointed up the Stony Rock Valley. 'Go there,' he snapped. 'Tell 'em, open up.' He added a snarl. 'Tell 'em, pronto. You understand? Muy pronto!'

The man inclined his head briefly. 'Sure thing, boss.'

He did not like to be spoken to like that. But, with Ted, you had to be careful — very careful. He had a temper that could flare up viciously for the slightest of reasons. And, if he took against you, you could easily end up with a knife in your ribs.

Ted watched the man ride off. But his mind was already elsewhere. He was listening again — hard, for the sound of another horse, above the muffled rumble of the cattle. But there was no such sound. Where the hell *was* he? He should have been there by now. The snarl on the face of the listening man grew greater. Well, he'd *better* be there, and soon! Or he, Ted Gonzales, would make damn sure that he regretted his tardiness.

At the top of Stony Rock Valley the lone rider was raising his voice. 'Open up,' he shouted. 'Pronto.'

A man's head loomed over the parapet. 'All right,' he growled. 'Give us time, will you! This thing don't move easy.'

'Boss man's in a hurry,' snarled the horseman. 'So move it! Quick.'

The head above the parapet disappeared, and soon, to the sound of much grinding and grating, the heavy rock in front of the horseman began to swing slowly towards him, to reveal the forms of three men pushing at it with all their strength. As it slowly swung, the watching horseman could see again what he had noticed many times before — that the heavy boulder was very delicately balanced — delicately enough for it to be moved in this way.

The men propped the boulder in its new position with a couple of rocks. Later on, when they moved it back again, it would take less effort than had been required to open it. In the meantime a passage way was open, narrow, but wide enough to let cattle through one at a time. Through this aperture now rode the big man with the dull eyes and the heavy beard — the one who had earlier, a day or two back, ordered the elimination of Texas Jake and Ramon Alvarez.

'Where's Ted?' he snapped.

The other merely pointed down towards the mouth of the canyon, and the big man moved his mount down carefully over the rocks.

Ted's manner when the man eventually reached him, was one of careful politeness. They had no liking for each other, but business was business, and each needed the other — Ted to do the work, and the rough stuff; the other man to do the thinking, the planning, the organization.

The big man glanced around. 'Steve and the others not back yet?'

Ted shrugged. 'Was shooting. Earlier. Them two sure holed up. Steve, the others, they finish the two. Then they come. Soon.'

The big man was looking round again. 'And our . . . friend?'

He spoke with a sneer. Ted scowled angrily. 'That hombre! If he not here pronto, I go fetch him.'

The other nodded, listening to the oncoming cattle, their forms now distinct in the bright moonlight as they approached, as were the forms of the two riders guiding the leading animals to the mouth of the valley. Once there, reluctantly, the cattle began to mount the little gorge in ones and twos, urged on by the two riders. Neither the beasts nor the riders took the slightest notice of the two watching mounted men. For the riders, and the watchers, it was all by now a routine. It had all been done so often before.

* * *

So intent were the two onlookers on watching the cattle go by that neither of them was aware of the arrival of the third horseman until he joined them at their silent vigil. Immediately they became aware of his presence it was the tall man with the beard who spoke first.

'Ah! Matt! We missed you. Thought

you had forgotten all about us — that you weren't coming, after all.'

His words were uttered in a mildly bantering, mocking tone. Matt Steadman said nothing, looking straight before him, his gaze stony.

'After all,' went on his tormentor, in the same mocking tone, 'as you know only too well, we require your presence at these little . . . ah, business transactions.' He chuckled gently. 'Your presence provides our operation with an aura of — shall we say? — respectability — even a sort of, well, legality almost.' And he chuckled again, more loudly this time.

Still keeping his stony gaze straight ahead before him, Matt Steadman spoke slowly and deliberately, choosing his words with care.

'There is nothing either legal or respectable about what is being done here now, and you are well aware of that, Jock Campbell. What you are engaged in here is theft, cattle theft, nothing less.'

The dark brows of the big man came down momentarily in a thick scowl. 'Come, come, Matt!' he said, with more than a touch of tartness. 'Those are rough words, quite uncalled for among . . . business associates, such as ourselves.'

Matt Steadman made no reply, maintaining his stony silence.

The other man's irritation swelled suddenly to anger.

'Thieves, are we? Cattle thieves? Well, *you* have had no objection to taking your share of our profits! You won't dirty your hands, but you are quite willing to share in the proceeds.'

Matt's words when, after a long pause, he eventually spoke, were again slow and deliberate, and chosen with care.

'My role in this whole enterprise has been despicable. You are quite right. I have shared in the proceeds of your thefts, and I must therefore share equally with you in your guilt.' He paused for a moment. 'No,' he said slowly, 'that is not right. Mine is the greatest guilt. For I have been robbing not a stranger but my own partner. And I have not only robbed him, I have also betrayed the trust he put in me.'

Ted Gonzales was scowling ferociously. But, before he could speak, Jock Campbell made a sign to him that he should remain silent.

Then Jock turned to Matt Steadman. 'You bother me, Matt,' he said softly. 'What is it that, suddenly now, you have on your mind?'

Matt slowly shook his head. 'It's something,' he said grimly 'that I should have had on my mind a long time ago. In fact, I should never have got into this whole thing.'

Jock Campbell looked at him, thoughtfully. 'But then,' he said at last, very quietly, with great menace, 'there were so many things that you should not have got into in the first place, weren't there?'

Silence. Stony silence in reply.

'I'm thinking,' went on Jock Campbell softly, 'for instance of — '

'You don't have to go on,' snapped Matt harshly.

'Oh yes, Matt, I really do. There was the matter of those rustled cows when you first started up, those cows that gave you your first break. Before, that is, you lost most of what you had built up, when you gambled in bank shares. Shall I go on?'

'You can do what you like,' snapped Matt. 'But I'm here tonight to tell you that I've had enough of your blackmail. This is the last drive that I take part in.' He turned and stared straight at Jock Campbell. 'I'm throwing in my hand, Jock,' he announced grimly, 'and you can make of that what you will. I'm pulling out of this whole dirty business — and I'm doing it right now, from this moment.'

Jock Campbell smiled gently and kindly at Matt. 'Oh dear, oh dear!' he said, with a sigh. 'When will you grow up? When will you face the real world — and come out of your juvenile dream-life?' His voice suddenly became harsh. 'What about all the other things you should not have got mixed up in? That bank robbery, for one.'

'I was dragged into that,' snapped Matt. 'It was not my choice.'

'No? Nevertheless, a man died. The teller, shot dead. Remember? Who did that? Your horse?'

'That was an accident,' snarled Matt. 'You know damn well it was!'

Jock Campbell grinned maliciously. 'So you say. So you say. But you know as well as I do there are no accidents in a bank robbery. That was murder, that's what it was. And you were going to swing for it — until *I* swore that you didn't do it. They hung young McLaren for that 'accident' of yours — remember?'

Matt now suddenly turned on Jock Campbell. There was viciousness in his snarl. 'I had no option, damn you! You *know* I had no option.'

'Ah, yes, I remember now,' said the

big man mockingly. 'The baby. You were concerned about your child.'

'It was Judith,' muttered Matt. 'That's all I cared about — what would happen to Judith.'

The other man smiled softly, menacingly. 'And now? What about Judith now? Now that you have decided to . . . withdraw from our mutual . . . business enterprise. What will happen to Judith now?'

Once again Matt Steadman swung round and faced his tormentor.

'Nothing,' he said grimly. 'Nothing will happen to her. *I'll* see to that!'

From behind the three horsemen, sharp in the clear bright moonlight, came a voice.

'Judith will see to that herself, thank you!'

It was Judith.

★ ★ ★

Matt swung round in the saddle, his face white with a mixture of fury, and fear for the girl. 'Damn you, girl!' he snarled. 'I told you to keep out of my affairs!'

Her reply was sharp, scathing. 'How *could* I keep out, suspecting all the trouble you had got yourself into?'

'I don't want you mixed up in this. Go back — now!'

But it was the tall man who spoke next — softly, mockingly. 'Too late, Matt. Too late for that now. Like it or not, she's in it.'

Matt swung round on him. 'You harm her, Jock — you do anything that will harm her in the slightest way — and I'll kill you. I swear to God I will. I will seek you out wherever you are hiding.'

Jock Campbell chuckled softly. 'Let's not get *too* dramatic, Matt. No harm will come to her, provided — '

'Provided *what*?' It was a vicious snarl.

The other chuckled gently again. 'Provided you behave yourself, of course.' Again he paused, thoughtfully

189

this time. 'For example, we are going to forget the little conversation we were having when we were so — opportunely, shall I say? — interrupted by your daughter.' Now his voice became even softer, full of menace. 'There's going to be no more talk of throwing in your hand, of getting out, of spoiling our very profitable little business.'

'I meant what I said,' grated Matt.

'Oh, sure, sure. Of course you meant what you said — at the time. Of course you did. But now you have changed your mind, haven't you?' Again the evil chuckle. 'Because, just to make sure that you really *have* changed your mind — and that it will stay changed — your daughter is going to spend a little time with us, as our guest, of course — an honoured . . . and valued guest.'

'You're intending to kidnap her? Is that what you're telling me?'

The tall man made soft, deprecatory sounds, clicking his tongue in disapproval. 'Your thinking is so crude, Matt. You use such ugly terms. Kidnap is a term

I would never think of using. No, as I said, Judith will be our guest — our honoured and valued guest, spending a pleasant holiday south of the border, in Mexico.'

'In *Mexico*!' It was a shout of disbelief from Matt.

'Good heavens,' said Jock, in mock surprise and disbelief. 'You talk as if Mexico is somewhere at the ends of the earth, whereas, as you well know, it is not all that many miles down the road from here — so to speak, you understand.'

'You're not taking her to Mexico,' snapped Matt. 'Under no circumstances are you going to take her to Mexico.'

Again the mock surprise from the other. 'Oh, dear! You have quite the wrong idea, Matt. No harm will come to the girl. None at all. She will, after all, at all times be under the care — the personal care — of our good friend Ted here. You can have no objection to *that* surely?' This time the chuckle was even more malicious.

'You are not taking her to Mexico,' grated Matt. 'You are not taking her any-damn-where!' Quick as a flash his hand went down on to the butt of his six-gun. But he was too late. The gun was only halfway out of the holster when the bullet from Ted Gonzales's weapon drilled a small, neat, round hole in the middle of his forehead.

For a moment there was silence, as Matt's body slumped down in the saddle, and then slowly slid off the horse to the ground. After that, the first sound was the piercing scream of Judith. In a flash, she was off her horse and at the body of her father, uselessly cradling his head in her arms. 'Murderer!' she shouted. 'Murderer! Murderer!'

But it was the soft viciousness of Jock Campbell's words that Ted Gonzales was hearing — not the screams and shouts of the distraught girl.

'You fool!' hissed the big man. 'You damn fool! You've killed the only insurance we possessed. You stupid, idiotic fool!' He looked briefly at the cattle still being herded up the valley.

'We'd better get out of here,' he muttered curtly. 'We'll have to leave the rest of the cows. Get the girl.'

Ted Gonzales dismounted and walked over to where Judith still cradled the head of her dead father. She was still shouting insults at him when he grabbed her arm. She fought him off fiercely. Suddenly his anger flared viciously, and he raised the quirt he held.

At that precise instant, as if this whole scene was merely the repeat of an earlier episode, the voice of Texas Jake came out of the moonlight behind Ted Gonzales.

'Just hold it right there,' drawled Jake — as he had drawled that other morning out in the desert.

★ ★ ★

Ted Gonzales wasted not so much as the fraction of a second. With the speed of a whiplash he jerked Judith to her feet and swung round to face Jake, the body of the girl effectively shielding him from Jake's fire.

'Now *hombre*,' he snarled. 'You shoot, you kill her first.'

But immediately, from a rocky outcrop behind Ted, came the voice of Ramon Alvarez, speaking in Spanish. 'You have three seconds, *bandido*, to release the *señorita* and thereby save your worthless rattlesnake life. *Uno, dos* — '

Like a hot brick Ted released Judith, moving a smart step back, and raising his arms with alacrity.

'Good,' said Ramon, still in Spanish. 'You were only just in time. There is nothing I would have liked better than to blow your poisonous head off your filthy shoulders. Put your hands on your head. Link your fingers.'

The man did so — again with alacrity. Ramon switched to English. 'You, too, *Mister* Campbell. My trigger finger is developing a sort of will of its own when I point my gun at you. I would be very, very careful if I were you.'

In the Stony Rock Valley the cattle were still following each other up the rocky slope. At the top the two riders were forcing them, in single file, through the opening in the parapet. Fortunately the riders had more than enough on their hands, and couldn't really see or hear what was going on with their two watching bosses — even if they had wanted to, Jake reflected. He moved out of his place of concealment among the rocks.

'Put your hands down, Ted.'

Slowly, cautiously, the big Mexican did so, his eyes darting suspiciously about, suspecting a trick. But there was no trick. Just Texas Jake standing there, silently, watching him. Gradually the man's confidence returned. Imperceptibly his stance began to alter until, after a while, it had become the posture of a gunfighter. On the balls of his feet, his knees slightly bent, his body inclined forward a little, his hands hanging down loose near the butts of his two six-guns — he was ready.

His eyes bored through the moonlight into the face of Texas Jake. This was *his* scene, a scene he, Ted, had so often — and always successfully — played before. And he would be successful this time, too! He would kill this gringo. Let the gringo make the slightest move towards either of his two guns and he, Ted, would shoot him — dead.

But the move that Jake made was not towards his guns. He, too, was on the balls of his feet, knees relaxed, shoulders a mite forward. And his two hands also hung loose and relaxed near the butts of his guns. It was the right hand that moved. But not towards the gun-butt! It moved away, slowly, outwards, the fingers opening and stiffening out from a flat hand.

Ted was suspicious. What the hell sort of a move was this — from a gunfighter? But the hand was going away — far away — from the gun-butt.

Ted waited to see what Jake would do.

When the hand, stiff-fingered still, was far out from the body, it stopped and began to come down — slowly — towards the gun-butt.

Ted almost laughed out loud with a mixture of relief and contempt. So the fool thought that he, Ted, was going to wait for him to reach the gun-butt.

The hand continued slowly on its way down towards the gun. Any moment now, and it would flash down with the speed of light, grasp the butt, bring the weapon out and up, the first bullets leaving the barrel as it emerged from the holster.

But Ted did not intend to let the process get that far! With Jake's stiff-fingered right hand still almost a foot away from his gun, Ted made his move. His right hand streaked down to his holster and grasped the gun-butt. It was a move made with matchless speed, and while Jake's hand was still inches away from his gun. In one continuous lightning motion the gun was coming up out of Ted's holster, and he had already started the first pressure on the trigger, when the unbelievable happened — Jake's three slugs struck him full in the centre of his chest.

Ted Gonzales fell to his knees. The shot from his gun, going off in the reflex squeeze of his trigger-finger, ricocheted off a nearby rock with a screaming whine. The red stain continued to spread rapidly over his chest, and he slumped to the ground.

Jake, both guns out, moved cautiously towards the dying man and kicked away the gun lying on the ground. Then he holstered his own guns, pulled out Ted's other six-gun and threw that, too, aside. Ted's knives Jake reckoned he did not need to worry about. The man was too weak, too near death, to use them.

Ted's lips were moving, the words coming faintly in a whisper. Jake put his ear near the face of the dying man. There were only a few words — bitter words — in Spanish. '*Zurdo*! I should have . . . guessed! — You are . . . left-handed!' The effort was too much. The man's head flopped suddenly to one side.

Ted Gonzales was dead.

10

Marshal Jim Birch stood, legs akimbo, his hands on his hips, looking down at the body of Ted Gonzales.

'Well,' he said at last curtly, 'that's one murdering robber we won't have to worry about ever again.'

A few yards away two men from his posse were tying the hands of Jock Campbell behind his back.

Jim Birch walked over to the man.

'Caught red-handed this time, eh Jock? Caught in the act. I reckon I've got all the evidence I need now for the circuit to put you in the pen for a good few years.'

Jock Campbell, a snarl on his face, said nothing.

'Put him on his horse. Tie his feet underneath. We're taking him along.'

One of the posse gestured up Stony Rock Valley.

'What about the others?' For the rest of the posse had ridden up the little valley after the rustlers. These latter, seeing that the game was now finally up, had tried to turn back the remaining cattle coming up the valley, and stampede them down against the posse. But the cattle had been too few, and the valley not narrow enough, to hinder the pursuers. At the top of the gulch two of the rustlers were trying desperately to move the rock back into place. But they had no time. The pursuit was coming up too fast. They dropped the poles they were using and fled through the gap to where their horses waited on the other side.

'What about the rest of the fellers?' repeated the man to Jim Birch, pointing once more up the gulch.

Jim looked up the valley.

A slow, grim smile formed on his face.

'They're busy,' he said. 'They'll come when they're through.'

He walked across to where Judith

crouched by the body of her dead father.

'I'm sorry it had to end like this for him.'

His words were sober. There was no false sentimentality in them.

She nodded briefly, dull with grief.

'I appreciate what you did,' said Jim, 'when you released me back there at the ranch house.'

She said nothing, just shaking her head in her grief.

'Can't think what was on Matt's mind,' brooded Jim. 'First kidnapping me. Then leaving me hog-tied at the ranch house. He must have been mad. It was an act of mad desperation.'

Still the grieving girl said nothing.

'Lucky,' went on Jim, 'that the posse came out looking for me. Just in time, too, to catch this lot red-handed.'

But Judith was not listening. Only her terrible loss mattered to her. About the rest she had no interest.

'What will you do now?' said Jim.

His words were kindly, and she made

the effort to drag herself out of her misery.

'I don't know,' she said slowly.

'I'll help,' said Jim. 'Any way I can. You know that.'

'Yes,' she said dully. 'Yes, I know that, Jim. Thank you.'

Jim turned away.

Jake and one of Jim's posse were putting Ted's body across his horse, tying it down.

When they had finished, they came across to do the same with Matt's body.

'No!' said Judith. 'No!' And then, as they stood back a moment, waiting, she added, distressed, 'Can't we . . . can't we carry him?'

Jake moved forward.

'No, ma'am,' he said gently. 'And he wouldn't mind. He lived on his horse.'

She shook her head and turned away, the tears coming now for the first time.

Jim Birch was riding off with his

escorted prisoner. As he passed Judith, he stopped.

'Forgot to mention,' said Jim. 'There's somebody waiting at the ranch house for you.'

She looked at him, surprised, puzzled.

'Somebody? For me? Who?'

But Jim merely raised his hand in a farewell gesture and urged his horse forward.

★ ★ ★

The ranch house and its out-buildings stood calm and peaceful in the bright moonlight as Jake and Judith, leading the two horses with the bodies tied on, rode up.

Jake dismounted and walked over to Judith.

'I'll put the bodies in the outhouse for the night. They'll be safe there. We can bury them in the morning.'

Judith nodded, glad to have the distasteful task taken from her.

'And leave your horse with me,'

added Jake. 'I'll see to him with the others.'

Again she nodded, giving him a weak smile.

'You've been very helpful,' she added, ashamed at the inadequacy of the thanks.

As she mounted the steps to the ranch house, the front door opened and a tall figure appeared, coming forward with hands outstretched.

It was James Longlater, her father's partner.

'Judith, my dear!' he said quietly, taking her hands in his. 'I'm so sorry, so terribly sorry.'

'Oh, Jim!' she exclaimed, falling into his arms. 'Oh, Jim! I'm so glad you have come!'

As the pair moved back into the ranch house, Jake walked over to the bunk house and roused a couple of the sleeping forms on the greensward.

Together the three of them put each of the bodies on to a rough plank stretcher, and covered each with a blanket, before laying them out in the shed.

Then they bolted the shed and unsaddled the horses, leaving the gear piled in the open on the grass.

Feeding and watering the mounts took some time. The animals had had a hard and busy day.

Eventually, when they had had their fill, they were let loose into the corral with the other horses.

The two men went back to their interrupted sleep. Jake unrolled his bed-roll, removed his hat, boots, and pants and slid gratefully into the bed-roll.

Within seconds he was asleep.

Epilogue

Ramon Alvarez had found his two deputies, who had come out with Jim Birch's posse.

Together, the three of them followed in the wake of the posse up Stony Rock Valley.

Now that their main quarry, Ted Gonzales, was dead, they still had another two of his henchmen to catch. They were both Mexicans, and both were wanted back in Ciudad Conchita.

However, Ramon was not optimistic about catching them. By now they must be far ahead of the posse, and riding hard.

Ah, well! No matter. It was Ted he had really wanted. Ted he would have moved heaven and earth to take back.

But Jake had saved him the trouble, and for that he was grateful. The other two? Well, if they caught up with them, fine. If not, it was back to Ciudad Conchita for all three of them, and no great worry about the fugitives.

The gang, after all, had now been broken. There would be no more rustling, and no more robbing of the *rancheros* round Ciudad Conchita.

The life of the marshal of Ciudad Conchita could henceforth return to normal — with more historical research than gang-busting!

He flashed a happy grin at his two companions and they, guessing well that he was thinking of going home, grinned back.

★ ★ ★

It was four days later that Happy Harry and his men rode back through the portals of the Palo Verde canyon.

While the cook drove the chuck wagon along to the cook house to unload all his supplies, and the other men went off to attend to their mounts, Happy Harry made for the ranch house to account for the cattle he had delivered to the trail-boss.

Happy Harry was inside the ranch house for considerably longer than usual, and when he came out his face wore a bemused look — almost as if he had been pole-axed!

It was the cook shouting that brought him back to the present.

'Hey, Harry! What am I to do with this stuff?'

'This stuff' turned out to be a pile of supplies, covered by a wagon sheet, in the body of the chuck wagon.

'Leave it,' said Harry. 'I'll look after it.'

He watered his horse, and turned it loose in the corral. Then he mounted the driving seat of the chuck wagon and urged the mules forward.

He still looked half pole-axed, but there was also a new eager anticipation that was beginning to grow in him.

It was an eagerness and an anticipation that Sarah noted with interest when the chuck wagon drove into Sweetwater.

'Hullo,' said Harry laconically, when he saw her. 'Brought the supplies you ordered.'

As he began to unload the wagon, her eyebrows arched up in surprise.

'All this, Harry?'

'Yep.'

'But I didn't ask for so much.'

'Never mind what you asked for. You need it, don't you?'

'Of course, but — '

'No buts. It's all here, and that's all there is to it.'

'But I can't pay for it.'

Happy Harry paused in his unloading and scratched his head.

'Well, how shall I put it? You don't have to pay for it.'

Sarah's brows came down sharply.

'You mean *you* — ?'

But he interrupted her. 'Not me,' he said.

'Then who?'

'The boss. The new boss. Mr Longlater. He reckons the Lazy B outfit owes you — that it owes you a lot more than this. So this is just a start.'

He smiled happily at the expression on the face of the bemused girl.

'Another thing,' he added, pulling his shoulders back. 'He's also made me foreman of the Lazy B!'

★ ★ ★

It was the following day that Texas Jake awoke in the pre-dawn cool of the desert morning.

The spot was the same at which he had been camping when he had first encountered Judith and Ted Gonzales, the small nearly dried-up seepage-spring with its remnants of grama grass, just enough for his two horses.

Jake watched the dawn growing in the sky. He made himself some breakfast, then he saddled the two horses and mounted the larger one.

Moving up on to the old coach trail, he looked across the valley the way he had done that first morning.

211

And this time he was surprised to see, once again, the plume of dust, signalling an oncoming rider. Only on this occasion there were no three following dust-clouds.

For a while Jake watched with idle curiosity.

This time the trap — for he could by now make out that it was a trap, with two occupants — was coming at a relaxed trot.

Still curious, Jake waited.

Soon he was able to distinguish that the two occupants were James Longlater and Judith.

James pulled the trap up as it drew level with Jake.

'Thought you'd be back in Texas by now,' quipped James.

Jake grinned. 'I'm on my way.'

'It was a fine job you did,' said James, seriously this time. 'I appreciate it.'

'We both appreciate it,' chipped in Judith. 'We're most grateful.'

'Warn't nothing much, what I did,'

said Jake laconically. 'Would all most likely have come out much the same on its own, without me.'

'I very much doubt that,' said James. 'It was a fine, professional job you did. I've posted your fee to your bank. I've also added a bonus.'

'Sort of celebration gift,' said Judith. 'You see, we're on our way to El Pueblo to get married this morning.'

Jake grinned.

'I sorta thought that was on the cards. Good luck to you both — and thanks for the bonus.'

'Thank you, Jake,' said Judith. 'And there's another pair you can also wish good luck. Sarah and Happy Harry are also on their way, for the same reason.'

Indeed, across the valley, a new dust plume had made its appearance.

Jake bade farewell to the couple, and watched the trap disappear in the direction of El Pueblo. Then he turned his horse and, leading the pack-horse, struck out across the desert, away from the old coach trail. He would rejoin the trail later on. He had no wish to meet the other bridal couple.

There was more than a slight pique in him that Sarah, having been turned down by him, had been so quick to find another candidate.

But immediately he dismissed the matter from his mind.

Idly he began to wonder what his next job would be.

There was always someone, somewhere who had need of a gunslinger.

Other titles in the Linford Western Library

THE CROOKED SHERIFF
John Dyson

Black Pete Bowen quit Texas with a burning hatred of men who try to take the law into their own hands. But he discovers that things aren't much different in the silver mountains of Arizona.

THEY'LL HANG BILLY FOR SURE:
Larry & Stretch
Marshall Grover

Billy Reese, the West's most notorious desperado, was to stand trial. From all compass points came the curious and the greedy, the riff-raff of the frontier. Suddenly, a crazed killer was on the loose — but the Texas Trouble-Shooters were there, girding their loins for action.

RIDERS OF RIFLE RANGE
Wade Hamilton

Veterinarian Jeff Jones did not like open warfare — but it was there on Scrub Pine grass. When he diagnosed a sick bull on the Endicott ranch as having the contagious blackleg disease, he got involved in the warfare — whether he liked it or not!

BEAR PAW
Nevada Carter

Austin Dailey traded two cows to a pair of Indians for a bay horse, which subsequently disappeared. Tracks led to a secret hideout of fugitive Indians — and cattle thieves. Indians and stockmen co-operated against the rustlers. But it was Pale Woman who acted as interpreter between her people and the rangemen.

THE WEST WITCH
Lance Howard

Detective Quinton Hilcrest journeys west, seeking the Black Hood Bandits' lost fortune. Within hours of arriving in Hags Bend, he is fighting for his life, ensnared with a beautiful outcast the town claims is a witch! Can he save the young woman from the angry mob?

GUNS OF THE PONY EXPRESS
T. M. Dolan

Rich Zennor joined the Pony Express venture at the start, as second-in-command to tough Denning Hartman. But Zennor had the problems of Hartman believing that they had crossed trails in the past, and the fact that he was strongly attached to Hartman's Indian girl, Conchita.

BLACK JO OF THE PECOS
Jeff Blaine

Nobody knew where Black Josephine Callard came from or whither she returned. Deputy U.S. Marshal Frank Haggard would have to exercise all his cunning and ability to stay alive before he could defeat her highly successful gang and solve the mystery.

RIDE FOR YOUR LIFE
Johnny Mack Bride

They rode west, hoping for a new start. Then they met another broken-down casualty of war, and he had a plan that might deliver them from despair. But the only men who would attempt it would be the truly brave — or the desperate. They were both.